UNEARTHLY TALES FROM SPACE

JOHN SPARKS

Unearthly Tales From Space
All Rights Reserved
Copyright © 2013 John Edward Sparks
www.unearthly-tales.com

ISBN-10: 1631030043
ISBN-13: 978-1-63103-004-8

PRINTED IN THE UNITED STATES OF AMERICA

Table of Contents

Chapter One: Arseina's Visitors
Chapter Two: The Super Jump
Chapter Three: Mystery Ship
Chapter Four: Surprise Crisis Aftermath
Chapter Five: : Out of Frying Pan, Into Fire Surreal Visitations
Chapter Six: Message in a Bottle Reaching for the Stars (Again)
Chapter Seven: Robert's Paradox
Chapter Eight: Atlantis Rising
Chapter Nine Villains and Killer Clowns
Chapter Ten: : Surreal Visitations
Chapter Eleven Reaching for the Stars (Again)
Chapter Twelve: Redux of Project Blue Star, Fall, 1959
Chapter Thirteen: The Cat's Meow

Chapter One

Arseina's Visitors

Arseina: *Named after the god of endurance, thought to have helped the early Arseina civilization endure and survive that world's cold climate, in the year 01 (Twelve World Common Time) T.W.C.T or pre-T.W.C.T 36719.*

Guild historical addendum: The Twelve-World Federation was established in the year pre- T.W.C.T 36719. Arseina's native calendar appears to have been constructed with astronomical teachings from the gods. It was established in pre-T.W.C.T year 03 by observing Arseina's planetary rotations: 437 rotations to complete one solar year. In the year 01 T.W.C.T Arseina's first colony was granted self-governance. This was when the Twelve-World Federation compact was agreed to, naming Alerium, the city of enlightenment, as the capital city of the Twelve-World Federation. This action was taken despite the fact that no new suitable worlds had been found for settlement.

Guild historical records

The World of Arseina

A freezing wind blew through Alerium, whistling past vast structures built up over hundreds of years. Anna watched snow falling. It snowed on an average of 200 days in Arseina's 437-day year. As Anna Urisa observed the never-ending winter weather, she felt warm and secure. She stood, silently monitoring the city below from her favorite platform.

Anna Urisa stood on a busy Guild observation platform overlooking the center of Alerium, her home city. Alerium, the capital of the planet, Arsenia, was commonly called "the city of enlightenment." From her vantage point Anna could see a vast cityscape—central spires of government buildings.

Alerium had been the Guild's capital of the Twelve-World Federation for over three hundred years. Today the capital existed, not only as the core of Arseina, but as the heart and soul of the twelve worlds. Anna reflected on this city; it had always been the center of her life. Alerium bustled with activity, both on the ground and in the sky. Anna felt she knew this city. Everything moved under its own power, even the middle of winter, even in the dead of night. At that moment the city hummed with a vibrancy that made Anna feel it was alive.

As she watched the space traffic come and go from the city's spires, she couldn't help but recall a dark chapter of her life. Anna's life had been formed in the heart of light and shadow, then hardened in the fiery forge of this city. Her existence revolved around this sacred oasis in an otherwise frozen world. Anna knew that even this observation platform was a part of the person she had become.

She could feel early childhood memories existing in tandem with her current view of the city. As far back as she could remember people had called Alerium "the city of enlightenment." Its traditional architecture—the Guild's finest—could be seen stretching to the horizons. As Anna stood observing the spires she could find no end to them. Some said the city spread so far in every direction that even the day-long path of the sun couldn't encompass its limits. Anna recalled vivid images of her mom, lovingly watching Anna scamper about the observation deck, trying to see the whole city at the same time. Now she watched as a silent city pulsed with light and life. She put her memories away.

After all, no one can live in the past, Anna thought to herself. *Or can they?*

"Lucky Landing Platform 37"—that was the nickname given to the platform nearest her. Over the years ships coming in from successful deep space missions always wanted to land there. No one was quite sure why. Whatever the reason, they started calling the place "lucky." Maybe it was just because not all ships returned. Anna stared down at it, and felt a shiver of pain. The source of the pain was something that had happened right there at that spot. For Anna it was anything but lucky.

The last time she'd visited this perch was fifteen years ago. Now the memory brought tears to her eyes. It was like muffled whispers in a crowded room. A large part of her wanted only to blot out the past, but she knew the links between past and future, and that forgetting could sometimes be fatal.

"Mom," the child, Anna, chirped, pulling on her mother's dress, "Mom, when is Dad going to be home? Mom? There are some men here to talk to us."

Her mother didn't answer. Instead she stared at the men at the door—Guild officials, faceless, nameless creatures of bureaucracy. One of them gave Anna's mother a note, said some apologetic words, and left. Her mother had stood at this very spot. She'd angrily shouted after the men, but they hadn't looked back. Then she'd begun to sob. Little Anna only recently had learned to read. She hadn't understood the full meaning of the note, but she'd recognized words. Years later she could still recall the first time she'd seen that document, with its official-looking print: "Guild Memorandum 152, The Guild hereby declares Guild Scout Ship *Urisa*, missing, along with all ship personnel. Probability of return: negligible. Search perimeters: unknown." Even before she could comprehend the meaning she'd memorized the words. It was hardly necessary. She'd eventually retrieved the document from her mother's files, and now she carried it with her. It was there as she looked out at the landing platform.

Though she was still reliving the past, Anna stood in that spot at a moment when she was launching herself into an unknown future. Behind her were those grim childhood days when their hopes had burned dimly, then hardly at all. Days turned into weeks. Little information came in, and what did come offered only false conclusions. It was hard to think of him as dead, but time broke down memories, making it difficult to imagine him alive either. What would her father think? She had to believe he would be proud.

Though the ship on the landing platform wasn't her father's it would carry the family name. Guild law gave captains the right to name their command ships after themselves, so her ship would be Guild Scout Ship *Urisa*, just as his had been. She reached into her pocket and anxiously felt another much newer sheet of paper. A large silver ship taxied into Platform 37. Her fingers traced the words on the paper: her command transfer letter. Its orders were the key unlocking a 15-year-old mystery. Anna wiped a tear from her eye. *If only Mom were here.*

Anna's mother had never recovered. She'd died just a few years after his disappearance. Anna had told her mom she would find him somehow. Now the city of enlightenment was giving Anna a chance to fulfill that promise. She turned away from the ship, turning to the widest vistas of the city. This would be her last look at Alerium, her last memory of home. When Anna looked out into the city, the image of how densely populated it was filled her mind. She loved Alerium's look and feel—densely populated buildings of steel and glass, rising hundreds of stories into the sky. The city was history rising from the ground. Guild architecture had evolved from academic traditions. Stone and brick had given way to precious metals and transparent polymers, with a vertical aspiration to touch the stars. The spires often did touch the clouds. Even now, whenever the stars were visible, Anna automatically searched them for clues of her father. The architecture, with its clerestory windows and pointed arches, seemed to speak to the same problem. In Anna Urisa's mind finding her father still seemed possible.

Captain Urisa stood aboard her newly assigned scout ship, ready to take command. She would take her place among the many, past and present, honoring the Twelve-World tradition.

"Today, in the time-honored tradition of the Guild, I honor every captain that lived before me," she told the officers assembled on the command deck. "With this cup we bind our unity as a family. Drink and be as one." She poured a bottle of wine into a large silver chalice.

As the crew passed around the cup of unity, Urisa took her place in the captain's chair. Seeing a bank of switches on the arm of her chair she chose one. A standardized Guild command console appeared, listing all ship systems. She accessed communications. Holding her command transfer letter, she placed a call to the Guild's ship registry office. A lady with long braided hair, wearing the Guild's standard uniform, appeared on the screen.

"Guild Ship Registry, give me your ship's I.D. number and command authorization code," she said in a dry monotone. Urisa felt a surge of excitement as she readied herself to call the ship after her own name.

"Registry ship I.D 000 Guild Scout 45, authorization code is Guild 37, department 17." Urisa waited for a response. She had preferred the old system where universities had names, not numbers. It was a pointless preference. The Twelve Worlds had thousands of universities now, and numbers solved many problems involved with identification.

"Captain, the name of your ship is now registered the Guild Scout Ship *Urisa*. Activation of your command codes in thirty seconds."

The lady paused for a second, her face suddenly reflecting true emotion. "Anna, find him," is all she said, locking eyes with the captain before ending the call.

"Guild Ship Registry out."

The abrupt end of the call left the captain alone with her thoughts. She was about to travel beyond the twelve systems the Guild had settled.

Captain Urisa turned on the forward view screen, overlooking the landing platform on level 37. Arseina was a cold planet, featuring more snow than anything else. On the platform snow swirled, drifting into piles. The silvery bow of Anna Urisa's new ship reflected the falling flakes. The drifts on the landing platform offered no threat, but she enjoyed watching the snow. A cold shiver ran up her spine. *Could this really be the last time?* She wondered, then she closed her eyes and shook off the feeling. She made her mind into an island of stability; all feeling of worry and insecurity melted away. Breathing deeply she sat, her mind at peace. Energy surged through her body while her eyes remained closed.

Finally it was time. With a touch of a finger she activated the ship intercom. "Captain Urisa to First Officer Onno."

After a slight delay the voice of her first officer came back. "First Officer Onno here, Captain."

"Onno, is our new crew member on board?"

"Yes, Captain, he is in his quarters. Do you need him?"

"No, as you were, Onno. Just wanted to know if we could shut the doors and prepare for takeoff."

"Yes, Captain, everyone is set. All provisions are aboard."

"Roger that, Captain Urisa out."

She deactivated the intercom, and glanced outside one more time. The wind was picking up, blowing the landing pad clear. She remembered her first mission off-planet, years earlier. On that earlier winter day she'd stumbled across a snow-covered landing platform, hurrying to report for duty. After students completed the necessary classes on land, the Guild required them to go off-world, where they would work in their field of study. Students spent several years doing this, earning their membership in the Guild.

When Anna had been a student she'd heard all the space stories about the early days of faster-than-light travel. That had led to the current Guild system. They'd found a once-occupied world missing its inhabitants, yet full of resources and advanced technology. Soon other worlds were discovered, and the universities became a natural training ground for skills in every discipline.

Anna thought of checking with Commander Onno about his training activities for the Guild students, but decided it could wait. Instead she contacted Chief Engineer Orto on the ship's intercom: "Captain Urisa to Chief Engineer Orto."

"Chief Engineer Orto here, Captain."

"Prepare for cold start."

"Roger, Captain, Engineering stands ready. Cold start protocols loaded and ready for activation."

"Roger. Engineering proceed to start up."

"Yes, Captain, the board reads green, initializing primary reaction," said the Chief Engineer.

Orto monitored the reactor control systems as they indicated primary initialization inside the reaction chamber.

"Captain, reaction is holding at five percent."

"Thank you, Engineering. Bring the reactor to flight mode and stand by."

"Reaction is now holding at thirty-five percent. Engineering standing by, as ordered, Captain."

Anna activated the ship-wide intercom, "All hands, this is the Captain. Prepare for takeoff. Helm, switch to internal power and disengage umbilical." Her even voice hid her excitement.

"Roger, Captain. Switching to internal power and retracting umbilical."

Captain Urisa watched her new helm officer work quickly.

"Umbilical has retracted, Captain," the officer reported. "The hatch is secure."

"Excellent," Urisa said.

The helm officer was a new Guild member, earning her navigation credentials on multiple trips outside the twelve worlds.

Here on her first command Captain Anna Urisa held her crew to strict operation protocol. She turned to the first officer standing by her side.

"Commander, are we ready for take off?"

"Yes, Captain; I visually verified that the hatch is sealed and locked, the rector is operating properly and holding at thirty-five percent, all equipment is stowed away properly, and the crew's morale is high."

"Thank you, Commander, the honor is all yours."

"Roger, Captain, the honor is mine."

The Captain rotated the command console over to her first officer. With an experienced hand he activated communications quickly, calling up an appropriate channel.

"Arseina Port Authority, this is First Officer Onno of the Guild Scout Ship, *Urisa*."

"Scout Ship *Urisa*, this is Arseina port authority," said a voice over the command deck intercom.

"Roger, Port Authority. We are seeking clearance for planetary exit at this time."

"Scout Ship, *Urisa*, your skies are clear. Proceed to orbital insertion and good luck, *Urisa*. Arseina Port Authority out."

Captain Urisa grinned. "Good job, Commander. Now comes the part I've been looking forward to since I was a kid watching ships taking off and landing." Her eyes softened for a moment, looking dreamy, then it was back to business. "Helm, bring us to positive one percent buoyancy."

"Roger, Captain, positive one percent buoyancy achieved."

The ships antigravity generators slowly came online, allowing the ship to gently rise above Landing Platform 37.

"Helm, take us to positive five percent buoyancy and retract the landing gear when we clear the landing platform," she ordered. "Maintain at five percent until we clear the observation tower on thrusters only."

At Helm was Second Lieutenant Uanne, a new Guild member from one of the agricultural districts on Arseina. Anna had found her to be one of the most talented navigators around. During her Guild training years Uanne had been required to calculate jump variables to an unknown star with no technological help—entirely within her mind. Uanne hadn't flinched, coming up with the correct numbers. Anna admired her new officer. It took most Guild navigators years beyond their training to master unaided jump calculations.

"Roger, Captain," said Uanne. "We are at negative one percent and the ship is rising. Landing gear is retracting."

The ship rose without effort, leaving behind undisturbed snow. It drifted up through snow and wind, passing multiple observation platforms. Visitors in the observation platforms watched snow swirling, sticking, then reflecting off the ship's mirror-finish exterior.

They were seeing a ship built from a standard Guild design, capable of operating for long periods in extreme environments with crews ranging between fifteen and fifty. Long-range scout ships like Urisa were meant to be sleek and fast, sporting a spear-shaped design with rounded curves and powerful engines.

As the ship rose above the last observation tower, Helm continued to update the Captain: "Landing gear is secure. We will enter the cloud layer in twenty seconds, ten seconds, five seconds, visibility is now zero. Sensors indicate the sky well above us is clear, there is no traffic in our area."

"Very well, Helm, take us to one hundred percent on the positive buoyancy," said Anna.

"Roger, Captain, bringing positive buoyancy to one hundred percent."

As the ship accelerated through the clouds, Anna said: "Helm, bring the sub-light engines online and take us out at best possible speed."

"Roger, Captain, sub-light engines are online, we have achieved escape velocity and continue to accelerate."

"Thank you, Helm. Stand by for jump coordinates."

"Roger, navigation computer is standing by for coordinates," reported Lieutenant Uanne.

Anna looked at her executive officer, Onno, standing next to her. Leaning close, she said in a hushed voice: "Have you looked over the data on the three worlds we've been assigned?"

"Yes, Captain," he breathed.

"Good, good." She paused. "I'm thinking, some of the crew is new, and most haven't worked together on this ship. Maybe we should start out with the first system in the Guild report. Give them time to settle in and adjust to the new command."

"I believe that to be the best course of action," Commander Onno said, maintaining a strong Guild discipline while addressing his Captain.

"Agreed," said Anna, pulling up the data on her command console. "Onno, take us to midway jump station; notify me when we are ready to make the jump."

"Yes, Captain. Anything else?"

"No, no. I think that should be it for now. I will be in my office looking over the probe data. Commander, the Command Deck is yours."

"Understood. Helm, set course for Midway Jump Station," Onno said firmly.

"Roger, Commander, setting course for Midway Jump Station."

"Captain's log, page one of new command, T.W.C.T Year 373 P.R. [planetary rotation] 171 of 437. I have taken command of Guild Scout Ship 45, now known as *Urisa*. The ship is on course for Midway Jump Station 1. Decision taken to jump to sector 8 Quadrant 4 Region 17 Star 14. Satellite data is inclusive. On the subject of value, it is hoped that Star 14 will be easiest on the crew, giving them time to adjust to a new command and practice their skills for more crucial worlds. End of planetary rotation log."

Captain Anna Urisa completed her first entry in her mission log, then sat back, putting her feet on her desk. Centered in the middle of her office, a holographic projection of the Star 14 system took up most of the room. As a mission began, it was the hope of every captain to find the world with the greatest profit. Anna watched data roll by as a projection of a habitable world appeared around Star 14. Probe data revealed little, except one highlighted area. A review of the data vaguely concluded: "Anomaly detected; no further data."

"If nothing else, maybe a mineral survey will keep us from leaving empty handed," Anna sighed, making a note in the database. "Guild paying five percent of total value to all responsible in locating mining opportunities for the Guild."

She flagged the data for further study, sent the message to all ship departments, and powered down the projector.

Chapter Two

The Super-Jump

Midway Station One: *Established in the year 7 T.W.C.T to provide safe navigation between Arseina and the first member of the Twelve-World Federation, **Turanno.** Turanno was settled in the year 36707 pre- T.W.C.T. It is named after the male god of fertility, who is believed to have fathered the first inhabitants of Arseina. It has a temperate climate, and its agricultural products are its primary export. Turanno helps to stablize Arseina's population growth and allows for increased industrial output, encouraging further outward exploration of surrounding space.*
Guild Historical Records

Commander Onno studied the scout ship's approach to Midway Station One.

"Helm, full stop," he said. Onno understood the needs of the mission. Jumping from star system to star system was inherently dangerous and good crews needed time to prepare.

"Roger, Commander. Full stop in thirty seconds... fifteen... ten... five seconds... and Helm registers full stop."

"Thank you, Lieutenant. Take station at navigation and signal Midway Station Fourteen, located in Sector Eight, Quadrant Four, Region Seventeen."

Looking forward to her first mission as a full member of the Guild, Uanne activated the ship's Midway communications terminal. "Sir, receiving Midway's subspace message. Stand by." Uanne studied new information from Midway Station Fourteen. The ship's navigation terminal revealed three new comets and five asteroids, all traveling outside the path of Midway. Uanne whistled as she reviewed the data. A class four solar flare emerged, demanding Uanne's attention. Utilizing one of the best navigation computers in the fleet, she plotted an intersecting jump into Star Fourteen's Midway Station. Timing was critical,

"Commander, calculations complete, course is set," she said,.

"However, I recommend we jump soon to make our window," she said, feeling the weight of her responsibility. Commander Onno watched from the captain's command console.

Guild Fleet Directive 5 alpha,
Excluding extreme emergencies, all jumps require executive review.

Onno examined data coming in from Midway station fourteen. He was determined to prevent a jump failure anywhere along the charted route. He understood the greatest risk to ship and crew was dropping out of subspace short of Midway. All Guild ships communicate using electromagnetic wave propagation, traveling at light speed with an effective range of two light years. Experienced crews understand one thing; if a ship is in distress, cosmic background can be a killer. A message going outside the two-light-year boundary has little chance of reception. Onno addressed his mission's risk with strength and an eye for detail, but he longed for the day when the ship would have a subspace relay onboard.

On the wall beside the Captain a com panel vibrated with the voice of her first officer: "Captain Urisa?"

She responded quickly, touching the com panel. "Go ahead, commander."

"Captain, the ship is prepped for jump."

"Roger, be right there," she said, confident that the first jump under her command would be a success.

With the great hope of fifteen years at hand, a thought worked its way through her mind. She focused on the potential for profit. Make the ship profitable and a crew would follow you to the ends of the galaxy; fail and... She regarded failure as unthinkable. Anna wanted the love and respect of her crew, but her primary aim was finding her father. She hoped they would be with her on that.

Finally she gave her command: "All hands, all hands, this is the Captain. Prepare to jump." She sat in her command chair, her legs crossed, as she leaned in the direction of Onno. Ready to give the order, Anna Urisa paused for a half breath. Commander Onno nodded his head, and looked at her. He approved. As soon as she saw his approval she gave the order: "Jump!"

Uanne had reoccupied the helm station only seconds before the jump command. An active ready light above the jump key started flashing, indicating executive approval for the jump. Her heart raced as adrenalin filled her body. When she reached for the jump key, she could see the ready light flashing a repeating triple green pattern.

Grabbing the jump key she counted down. "Jumping in three, two, one. Jump drive engaged." She turned the key.

Bristling with power, and separating from Midway Station One, the ship surged forward into a vortex of bright blue energy. All contact with the outside world stopped, and the stars and Midway Station One disappeared. Those sights were replaced by a blue smoke-like haze enveloping the ship. Captain Urisa knew what was next; a massive distortion wave emanated from the jump drive, traveling bow to stern. She braced herself. As the ship entered subspace every section and crew member endured this wave. It was over as soon as it started.

Anna moved gracefully through subspace, encircled by energy vortices pulsing with blue and white light. She could feel the jump drive's pattern pulsating as if the ship were a living being. In years past she'd walked the hallways in obscurity, touching the walls and feeling the life of the ship grow stronger as she approached Engineering. She'd wondered if that feeling was like that of taking a lover. Now that rhythmic pulse of jump drive energy throbbed like a heartbeat. Anna wanted to get up, walk through the ship, feeling the life in the walls, but the ties of her command held her like chains of iron.

Light years now separated the ship from Midway Station One. Arseina and its sun became a distant pinpoint of light. As the ship drove through subspace, Anna became restless. The normal monitoring of the command deck slipped further and further from her mind. She crossed and uncrossed her legs repeatedly, as she stared at the forward view screen showing the subspace vortex. It pulsed in a rhythmic pattern from the jump drive. She was lost in another world until her first officer, Onno pulled her back.

"Hungry?" he asked.

"What?" she murmured.

"Hungry... are you hungry?"

"I...uh...oh, maybe I am," she said. She realized she was back on the command deck.

"We still have about a day before we come out of subspace."

"Alright, I think I am hungry," she said.

She started from the command deck, only to stop short when she realized Onno wasn't with her.

"Alright, it was your idea so... come alone, will you?"

"Roger that, Captain," he said with a grin. The two walked to the captain's mess. Before they entered Onno stopped the Captain. "Back there on the command deck, you seemed lost in thought."

Anna chuckled and looked into his eyes. "I shouldn't tell you. You'll think I'm crazy."

"I know you're crazy, but that has never stopped me from serving under you before."

Anna looked away, feeling childish. "I was thinking about walking barefoot through the ship while I watched the vortex pulse outside."

Onno laughed lovingly, and heard Anna chuckling at herself.

"That's a new one," he said, recalling a day when they were both junior grade officers. He'd caught her down by engineering.

"Keep it quiet, mister, and I will reward you for your silence," she said, looking back up at Onno's eyes and giving him a seductive wink.

Onno smiled back as they entered the captain's mess.

Over the years they'd respectively served for and under each other, periodically changing places, but everything had changed one day, early in their careers, when he'd found her outside engineering. She'd stood, half-naked, pressing her face and hands against a bulkhead. She'd been walking in her sleep, and seemed to have stopped here just to sob. Anyone else that day might have reported her. It could've ended her career. But Onno knew better. His uncle had served aboard the *Urisa* under her father. This elder relation had asked Onno to keep a close eye on Anna, and Onno always had. The night he'd found her, she'd rewarded his silence in a way that helped her relieve her extreme loneliness. It was a loneliness she couldn't quite endure.

The ship continued through space, cutting through the light years until only a few remained. Midway Station 14 was in orbit around a red dwarf star in Sector 8. Under a Guild contract Arseina Spaceworks had sent out Midway Station 14 years earlier. The move had opened Quadrant 4 to further exploration.

In the early days of Guild exploration the mapmakers had divided the galaxy into 32 sectors. The intent of the move was to make mapping easier during exploration. Charting and mapping took on a bottom-up approach: find 20 stars, grouping them into a Region. When there were more than twenty, it was time to start a new Region. Soon the regions in Sector 1 numbered in the millions. The Guild then introduced quadrants, dividing sectors into four parts. This helped ships report their locations more accurately, as in Region 14,135,872 and Star 5. In the Guilds 300-year history, only 7 sectors had been successful explored.

Anna relaxed in the captain's mess, until a ship-wide alarm sounded. Command terminals throughout the ship started flashing red, displaying distance and time.

"Warning, proximity alert," said the computerized voice. "One light year warning is now in effect. All hands to their stations."

The Captain hurried out of her private mess hall and into the commotion aboard ship. The vibrations of the ship's subspace engines lost their rhythm, changing from a steady beat to a long drawn-out pulse. The vibrations slowed even more, finally ending completely after one last faint pulsation. Normal space appeared and with it Midway Station 14.

The ship slowed as it approached the station, scanning the area as it approached.

"Good job, everyone. Helm, give us a clean sweep of the area."

"Roger, Captain, starting sensor sweep." Uanne activated the ship's long-range sensors. A short-range scan ran continually for navigation, but long-range had a different purpose.

"Helm, report," the Captain ordered. Uanne worked quickly, mapping out the area while looking for anything of interest.

"Scanning, Captain. Midway is showing clear, no uninvited guests, second sweep in progress. Still no evidence of visitors in system."

"Very well, Lieutenant. Keep running active scans and engage the sub-light engines, take it nice and slow and give us a good approach on everything in system until we reach our primary target."

"Roger, Captain. Bringing sub-lights up to one-third, and setting course for outer system. Our course will take us to our target destination in thirty-one standard days, T.W.C.T." Star 14 was a red dwarf with five planets and an asteroid belt in its extreme outer region. The course brought the ship over a long ballistic arc from the outer ring of the system to the inner planets, scanning and studying every planet, moon and asteroid, looking for anything of value.

Anna scanned the sensory data, relieved at the news of no visitors. Midway stations served multiple functions. More than just a communication terminal with the home world, it was a station in its own right. Sometimes they were permanently manned, serving as ship repair yards and logistical ways in and out of system. The idea of it serving as a lifeboat didn't escape her either. Her mind drifted back to the story she'd heard from a retired captain. He told of a situation years earlier.A Guild scout ship answering a midway station's distress signal, was intercepted by some unknown entity. Apparently whatever stopped the ship either destroyed it, or made it vanish without a trace. Guild news networks ran the story about the altercation for days, but never mentioned that both ship and crew were now missing in action. That never made it into the official story.

With her keen understanding of the vast dangers of space, Anna shivered at the thought. With her crew ready and the *Urisa* moving into a search pattern Anna turned to her first officer. She wasn't surprised to see his proud grin. The crew's smooth functioning was largely the result of his training.

"You ready?"

"Ready and standing by, Captain," he said.

Both of them understood that training issues were seldom routine, and always serious. With a shortage of trained Guild members, the pressure to train and advance new members was growing every year. At least half of the crew was still being coached for Guild membership. Every position on the ship had a Guild member and crewman-in-training, assigned to every post. Commander Onno had followed up with every department, leaving bridge training last. There, Second Lieutenant Uanne knew little about training, but her knowledge of her tasks was second-to-none. When Onno had asked her to take a new crewman under her wing, Uanne felt a sense of pride. She would give her best to the honorable task of training a new crewman.

As Guild ship *Urisa*, slipped deeper into the system, Uanne started seeing a pattern. Something was showing up in the sensor sweep every few cycles--a "ghost" Commander Onno had called it, meaning that sensory data could be reflected back to the ship from elements in space or from worlds not yet charted or measured.

"Helm, bring us in," said Commander Onno as he scanned the screens. "Drive the ship deep into the system and let's see what kind of data we can get."

"Uh… driving it in deep, Commander?" Uanne queried, uncertain how to repeat the command.

"Yes, you'd better; it was your idea, Lieutenant. Besides, it's time to stretch our legs."

"Roger, Commander," Uanne replied. "Increasing acceleration toward our primary target." "Thank you, helm," said Commander Onno.

Uanne set a course for the second planet out from the red dwarf. Early scans of the world showed it was habitable: a large desert world, almost twice the size of Arseina. Uanne recalled the words of her first Guild instructor. Pounding his fist on the desk he would say: "Adventure equals profit, profit is found in the outer reaches of space. Your greatest adventure will be the challenge of yourself."

"I never really understood what that meant," she said to herself. "I am out here as a full Guild member, but…." She never completed the thought.

Chapter Three

Mystery Ship

Uanne's recollections were cut short when her navigation board came alive. "Captain!" she cried. "Contact, I am reading a ship in system, wait... Correction, I am reading a Guild transponder."

"What ship is it?" Anna demanded.

"Stand by, Captain, something is not right." Uanne stopped, not knowing what to say next.

"Helm report, Lieutenant!" Anna ordered. She saw Uanne freezing up. "Onno, help her." As Anna activated her command terminal, Onno jumped up, but stopped when the Captain switched on the main view screen.

"What ship is that?" Anna asked, pointing to the screen. What she was looking at wasn't a ship; it was a field of wreckage. When no one answered she gave a command: "Helm, all stop."

"Roger, Captain, all stop."

The Captain sat forward, staring, her fingers gripping the arm of her command chair.

"Commander, take the shuttle, Chief Engineer Orto, and Uanne and find out what ship that is. I want to know what happened out here."

"Yes, Captain," Onno said, then he snapped: "Uanne."

"Yes, Commander."

"I hope our helmsmen-in-training is up to the task; have him take over while we sort through... through... that out there."

Captain Urisa feared the worst. This could be the answer to a question she'd been asking for so many years.

"It could all be there," she thought, gritting her teeth. "What will I do if it is?" She sat frozen, afraid to move, fearing any wrong action. The truth might be something she wasn't ready for.

"Captain," came the steady voice of her first officer and friend.

"G-Go, ahead, Commander," she said, nearly faltering.

"Captain, this is not it--not the ship you're looking for," Commander Onno reported from *Urisa's* shuttle.

A sharp sound blared from the radio. Onno shrugged.

Anna let go a loud sigh. "Uh, ok so what can you tell me?" Anna shifted and focused the image, revealing the shuttle weaving through floating debris.

As the shuttle approached a large piece of wreckage, Chief Engineer Orto's voice crackled through the speaker: "Commander, I have located the source of the Guild transponder." He powered up a large multi-directional search light, then aimed it a larger, still intact section of the ship's remains. "There, see where mid-section is still joined with engineering," he said, shining the light on an intact docking port. "The transponder is broadcasting from that section; wait... Commander, sensor board is saying there may still be power there. Recommend we board and take a closer look."

"Agreed, stand by," said Onno. "Uanne take us in close but don't dock yet. Give me a three-sixty look."

"Roger, Commander. Engaging thrusters," she said. She maneuvered the shuttle so it appeared to be drifting, while slowly turning it toward the large section.

As the shuttle circled the wreckage, Orto ran the light down the length of the largest section. "There," he said, pointing at his main view screen. The shuttle turned and faced the backside of the fragment. Orto locked his light beam on what used to be the ship's interior. The light shone beyond the twisted metal framework, past remnants of internal super structure, to reveal a profound surprise.

"Right there, Commander," Orto called out. "Emergency bulkheads in place. Normally, that would mean nothing. Emergency Vacuum Seal—every ship has E.V.S stations throughout. This one's been manually applied. New ships have been experimenting with automated systems but never could it handle something like this!

Recommend immediate action. Still uncertain what happened, but those could be scorch marks on the outer hull."

"Agreed. Uanne, flip us around and initiate priority docking."

"Roger, Commander. I'm bringing the ship around now." As the thrusters reached full power, a bump rattled through the shuttle.

"Commander, take a look at this," Orto said, running the light over the top section of the ship as they passed it.

"I see it," said Onno. "That's starting to look grim."

The pattern of fragmented hull plating and scorch marks pointed to only one answer: The ship had been attacked by an unknown assailant.

"Commander," came the voice of Captain Anna Urisa, "we've started high resolution scans of the weapons damage. Early results may indicate-- Commander, are you ready for this? That ship may be over a hundred years old."

"Hundred! That's.... that's impossible..." Onno's voice trailed off,

"E.T.A on docking, Lieutenant."

"Stand by, commander, we don't want to scratch our shiny new ship on that old piece of junk."

"Uh.., oh, right," Commander Onno said, realizing the inevitable truth. "Over a hundred... can't imagine how one of our ships could have made it this far out."

At that moment Uanne's shuttle maneuvers rocked him almost out of his seat. While the shuttle positioned itself into docking alignment, Orto tried sending the docking protocol to the only intact docking port.

"Commander, auto dock is a no go, switching to manual, and extending umbilical."

"Roger, Chief. As soon as we have hard seal, suit up and join me at the docking port. Uanne, you have the shuttle; the Chief and I will be back soon."

"Roger, Commander," Uanne said, feeling a little uncomfortable at the thought of being left alone. The shuttle's umbilical had made a hard seal with the surviving ship fragment.

"Ready, Chief," Commander Onno said, standing at the airlock in his environmental suit.

"Yeah, uh, let's do it," the chief said.

Chief Engineer Orto Antium came from the farming world of Turanno. His earliest memories were of his father working the family company in orbit. They took in outdated, banged up, leaking ships. Past their operational life, most were employed in second-tier jobs that didn't require state-of-the-art technology. Functioning or not, when a ship arrived operators sought to wring out its last drop of value, salvaging all they could, then selling the parts. It was there that Orto had learned to the arts of salvaging.

As the Guild pushed deeper and deeper out into the frontiers, Orto found himself working the family dry docks, repairing and refurbishing old Guild ships, to help push them back into service. This became his main task. As the family business took on functions beyond that of a scrap yard, word of Orto's skills spread. Soon the Guild took notice. Skipping the normal Guild apprentice program, Orto moved straight into military training.

Commander Onno cycled the airlock, and started through the umbilical, only to suddenly realize his chief engineer wasn't with him. He buzzed Orto's earpiece. "Hey, wake up, man. You ok?"

"Uh, yeah, I was just thinking back to when I was a kid; we took ships like this apart all the time."

"Love to hear about it sometime, but for now the Captain is waiting."

Orto nodded silently, his mind bouncing off a memory. It was a veiled image he couldn't pin down.

The umbilical made a hard seal with the hatch from the surviving section. Orto examined the hatch, understanding they could pressurize the passage if they needed to. Uncertainty stopped him. The reality that the deadly vacuum of space might work as a firewall between a potentially dangerous ship and the shuttle couldn't be overlooked.

Orto examined the hatch. "Commander, judging by the degree of micro-pitting on this hatch, I'd say we can open it, but once we have, we may not be able to establish an airtight seal."

"Understood, Chief," said Onno. "Crack it open and let's move forward."

"Roger, Commander, stand by."

The outer hatch was recessed, allowing space in the frame between hatch and hull where an engineering port was hidden. Orto could use this to get information from the inside. Reaching for an access panel at the end of the shuttle's umbilical, he pulled out an interlink command cable, and plugged it into the engineering port. He hoped the controls for the airlock were still functioning. "Stand by, Commander attempting to establish a connection." He glanced at the readout displayed on the engineering data pad on his wrist.

"Hmm... no power to the airlock--attempting to compensate."

Orto examined his wireless connection with the shuttle's interlink computer, and extended a power cable to the hatch's engineering section.

Watching the result, he said: "Yes. Systems coming back online, Commander. Hatch is responding to my commands."

"Good job, Chief. Try to get it open."

"Roger, Commander. Sorting through the commands now. They're old, in fact, really old. I'm writing these codes from memory."

"Memory... how old is this ship?"

"Old, I saw a couple like it when I was a kid, and they were old then. We took one in for salvage but couldn't find any buyers for the parts."

"If it was useless, what did you do with it?"

Orto halted his work for a moment, as the episode came back to him. "The only thing we could do was to break it down to its frame, and rebuild it from the bottom up. Every collector in seven systems wanted it after they found out."

"Did you sell it?"

"No, it's still sitting in dry dock. It's a museum piece. As it turned out, it became more valuable to us than anyone else. We had it there on display, and all our customers were curious about it.

As word got out about the restoration, collectors started showing up, wanting their favorite ships restored. Who knew, right? That's what shifted our emphasis from salvaging to ship restoration. Soon we were rebuilding some of the Guild's top-of-the-line scout ships, and just about anything else that was getting some age."

"Wow, why are you out here? Sounds like you have more back home."

"Guild made an offer I couldn't refuse. In exchange for my teaching new engineers how to strip and rebuild in deep space, the Fleet sent Guild students to learn their craft working in the shipyards. New labor source, new ships being built... It's a win, win for everyone."

When Orto's data pad read green in the airlock menu he activated the hatch from his suit. "Ok, I am opening the hatch now."

Through the suit's communications line he could hear Onno's breathing. They waited for the airlock to open. Orto looked into Onno's eyes. "You ok, there?"

"What? Why do you ask?"

"Nothing really," Orto said, slapping Onno on the shoulder. "I just thought I heard some labored breathing. Was I wrong?"

"Ok, you got me. I'm a little pensive. Now get the door open."

"Stand by. Airlock is cycling now, Commander."

As the airlock started moving, they felt distinct vibrations through the environmental suits.

"Stand by, Commander," Orto said. "It's slow in responding." He realized that under a pressurized environment the screeching of metal on metal would be too much for anyone.

Watching his suit's data screen, Orto stepped forward into the airlock, ready to close the outer hatch.

"Commander, systems are starting to recharge and come online from the power transfer. According to the interlink computer, we have a positive pressure behind the inner hatch, with an ample oxygen supply, but..." Orto paused to study data flashing onto his screen. When he saw the temperature reading, he said:

"Closing outer hatch, and cycling the airlock. Recommend we keep our suits on the whole time...our flesh would flash-freeze if we left it exposed."

"Flash-freeze, got it, don't want that happening," Onno said.

"Stand by, Commander. The outer hatch is closing and we should be pressurizing momentarily." Orto watched the outer hatch move faster. As he glanced at his suit's interlink display, he heard Onno's muffled approval.

"I'm impressed," Onno said. "We have a hard seal on the outer hatch, no sign of a pressure leak. Inner doors opening, in three... two...one..." Inner doors opened, revealing a dark corridor littered with wreckage and personal effects. Commander Onno took the lead, using his suit's illumination system as he scouted out a safe path through the corridor.

"Hold up, Commander," Orto said. "I think I can bring up partial lighting. Power conduits are disrupted, but I'm attempting to redirect power through environmental, and... wait... got it."

Emergency light terminals came to life. Just as Orto began powering up, a nearby light bank exploded, showering the corridor with sparks.

"Ok, that is as much as I dare feed the system. Everything is unstable."

"Fine," Onno said. "Let's get moving."

The corridor shifted from graveyard darkness to a living land of shadows and light. They pushed deeper into the ship. The longer Onno pushed forward through dust and debris, the shakier he felt. The sound of his breathing echoed through his head. He craved more oxygen. As they moved through the corridor, dim lights flickered in silence.

"Orto."

"Yeah."

"You still with me back there?"

"Right behind you, Commander."

Onno dimmed his suit's lights, allowing him to see into the dust and debris without the glare.   Orto followed, considering

how to broach the subject of what he would need from the crew.
Suddenly Onno pitched backwards, arms and legs flailing. As he crashed into Orto, his boots lost their magnetic lock on the deck plating.

"Easy, Commander," said the Chief. "I have you. Just put your foot down... there. Now what's going on?"

"It was just, just... ok... I'm ok now, I found one of the crew. Up there," he said, pointing at a doorway that was no more than a zero-gravity jump away. "I'm sorry about that. I feel really embarrassed now. I knew they would be here. It's just... the place is a tomb and, anyway, it doesn't matter... Let's keep moving."

"Commander, wait."

Onno turned to his chief engineer. "If it's about me making a fool of myself, I'm sorry, I just...."

"Hey, no! It's not that, Commander," said Orto. Suddenly he realized this investigation was his to manage. "I need to access the crew members' suits, so I can upload all their data into our interlink computer, then make permanent copies. It's a manually loaded, century-old system, but I need to know what they said. Then we might understand what happened here."

"All right, Orto, take the lead," said the Commander. "Maybe we can wrap this up quickly." Onno stared at the wreckage. "I certainly wouldn't want to make this a permanent residence."

As Orto edged down the corridor, Onno stood fast. He aimed his light forward, hoping to provide better illumination for Orto.

"Commander," Orto said gently, "I need your help. Are you ready?"

Onno exhaled. "Alright, Chief, let's finish this."

"Luck of all luck," Orto said. "This guy was their engineer. It looks like he was setting up a lifeboat on this segment, but he couldn't finish in time."

"But they came pretty close," Onno said. The remains of the ship's crewman floated nearby. "What do you think went wrong?"

"I'll tell you all about it, Commander, but first I need your help. I'm going to place a recharge pad next to his suit's power storage unit. When that happens things may move fast. Once I've up loaded everything from his suit's memory core, he may have a remote activation code. That might trigger his suit's radio to signal the engineering terminal to power up. That would give us the ship's information. I think this was an information relay. He stayed here to make sure their prized possession would be available to anyone who got this far."

"Why do you think that?"

"Look at this setup. That low-level power signal we picked up came from right there." Orto directed a light beam into the room, highlighting a bulky and elaborate mechanism that spanned most of the room. "That, Commander, is a shuttle's reactor core on standby. A shuttle's identification transponder is designed for short range. Had the rest of the ship been intact we would have seen it the minute we jumped into the system. Their transponder signal would have bounced off every chunk of space rock out there. Stand by, Commander. When I power his suit up his internal lights will come on revealing his face. I recommend you and I both look away when that happens; it's not going to be a pretty sight. Oh, and one last thing: that engineering terminal there—when it comes online, ready your suit's interlink. Everything is over a hundred years old. If it comes online there is no telling how long it will last, so we need to move fast."

As Onno felt his confidence returning he said: "All right, Chief, this is your show."

Orto placed a small cylinder against one of the suit's recharge pads. There were several at key points on the uniform's chest and back. These were designed for suit-to-suit power transfer during an emergency rescue. As the cylinder activated, a disk-shaped device slid out from the end, forming a lock on the suit. "Charging," he said. "Minimal levels coming online, stand by...." Orto watched as a red light came on, and started flashing faster and faster. It turned yellow. "Minimal power," said Orto. "Accessing data memory core." Now the flashing was yellow. Orto worked his suit's data pad. "Reaching data core. Trans—uh—transfer in progress."

The flashing yellow light transformed into a steady beam.

"I'm in," Orto continued. "Data transfer under way, five percent, twenty, fifty-five, seventy-five... almost there, Commander. Stand by." A green light blinked on the emergency recharge unit. When the recharge was complete they heard a noise, followed by a radio burst. Orto pressed the green light, deactivating the unit.

"Almost done. His suit is powering up. Stand by... I got it... data transfer complete." Both men smiled feeling a rush of pride in their first success. Then the lights of the dead man's suit switched on.

"Oh!...uh, not good!" Onno groaned.

"Don't look, Commander," Orto said.

Both saw the face of death. Stumbling backward, they fought to regain their composure, but couldn't. This was Orto's prediction of the dead man's effect coming true.

Within moments the shuttle's interlink system signaled the reception of a transmission from the newly activated EV suit. Using his wrist interlink data terminal Orto raced to access the lifeboat's data.

"Commander! Reactor is coming online--fast, maybe too fast. We need to access that terminal in a hurry!"

Orto activated the inter-ship communication link, creating backup copies of everything they'd received. The lifeboat's lights starting coming online.

Onno viewed the terminal's readout. "Life support coming online," he reported. "I'm reading an energy surge in the main reactor--attempting to bring it down."

"Thank you, Commander. I'm disconnecting the umbilical's power transfer from here."

Orto worked his data terminal to its limit, accessing the lifeboat's data core and downloading a copy to the shuttle and scout ship while cutting the shuttle's power feed into the lifeboat.

"Chief, get over here," Onno warned. "You better have what you're looking for. This reactor is pushing its limits. Sub-zero temperatures didn't do their set-up any favors. Let's get going."

A power conduit exploded, showering them with sparks and smoke, as it almost knocked them off their feet.

"Stand by, Commander," Orto shouted into the radio. "Slow data upload. This is a huge library. We have to buy ourselves time."

"Ok, but see if you can shut this reactor down or, at least stabilize it." Onno shouted to be heard over the din.

Orto pulled up the reactor's interface on his EV suit. He didn't like what he saw. "Commander, there's no stopping it. The safeties never came online; if I only had all my tools... Anyway, we need to get clear."

"Roger. Let's go said Onno. "We'll download data as long as we can from the shuttle."

"Roger, commander." Orto stared at his data pad. It flashed a single phrase: "Data reference 1-through-12 found."

Orto worked fast to retrieve the data. "Let me save the data transfer, Commander. It could be essential." Without saying why, Orto started linking the reactor's control interface to his suit's data pad. "Attempting to redirect power and slow the reaction. I'm programming a macro into the reactor's computer so I can control it from the shuttle...it will only take a moment."

"Let's go, chief, before we're left behind."

"Ok, let's go."

Orto grabbed an emergency recharge unit and placed it on the crewman's suit. In one last motion he activated it. Finally the two men fled through smoky debris, and arrived back at the airlock. While the airlock cycled, Onno remembered seeing the placement of a second recharge unit.

"What's the second recharge unit for, if you don't mind me asking?"

"I needed a wireless relay station to control the reactor and the lifeboats' systems. I wrote a new program and uploaded it when we pulled all his data. The program will keep the recharge unit from transferring power until the suit has drawn down most of its juice...assuming the reactor hasn't gone critical."

They stepped into the umbilical. Orto opened the interlink port on the lifeboat. He waved at the commander to continue on to the airlock. "Give me a few seconds," he called. "Hold the door, I'll be right there." Orto accessed his connection to the lifeboat's systems. "Stand by, Commander," he said. "I'm uploading a work-around to the umbilical's interlink cables." Orto uploaded a program to control the data transfer through the dead crewman's radio. With a quick flip of his wrist he disconnected both cables. Finally he ran toward the airlock.

Orto activated the interlink system while he was running for the airlock. "Upload complete," he gasped. As the airlock cycled he added: "Link established—data transfer under way. Time to cut the cord."

Onno called up Uanne, "Fire up the thrusters and give us a minimum safe distance as soon as umbilical has retracted. Orto will give you the numbers shortly."

"Roger, Commander. Standing by."

Commander Onno and Chief Engineer Orto shed their EV suits, and rejoined Uanne. She was already pulling the shuttle away from the lifeboat. Onno took his place in the shuttle next to Uanne. Orto was close behind.

"Ok, Chief, it's your call now," said Onno said. He realized that if anyone could salvage the situation it would be the Chief Engineer.

"Ok, data transfer underway," Orto replied. "We're approaching twenty percent, with reactor pressure... climbing," Orto spoke haltingly, as new information poured in. "Stand by. I'm powering up the lifeboat's thrusters. Download signal is strong. Maintain this distance, Uanne. It's the signal's strongest zone for reception. We should be able to capture most of the download this way." He said nothing about the lifeboat's reactor.

His heart pounded, and his hands shook, as he applied safety devices to hold him in his seat.

"Lifeboat is on the move, attempting to compensate," Uanne said, driving the shuttle through the cloud of debris.

The shuttle followed the lifeboat through the wreckage. As the download continued, Orto worked feverishly to keep the reactor stable, hoping his efforts could squeeze out a little more data. "Oh boy," he breathed, as the download's final chapter started coming in.

He pushed the lifeboat's thrusters, knowing that might allow a little more time to get this last data. He worried that the lifeboat would start bouncing off all the debris. Knowing the risk, Orto hoped it wouldn't sting the shuttle pod.

"When I tell you to run for *Urisa*, drive this ship as fast as you can, Uanne. Got it?"

Uanne grunted her response as she dodged wreckage. Onno sat wide-eyed. At this speed avoiding debris seemed impossible, and some minor bits gave them glancing blows. A big enough chunk could easily smash them to bits.

The oncoming wreckage forced Orto to leave the download unmonitored so he could check for air leaks. Once, when he'd been young and overconfident, he'd been caught in a decompressing ship without a EV suit. Only his father's order that everyone carry a bottle of Emergency Vacuum Seal had saved him.

"Commander, we have a leak. Fixing it now." Orto took off his safety harness, and reached for the bottle of Emergency Vacuum Seal (Otherwise known as E.V.S.). when his station screen flashed red. The sound of an alarm filled his ears. Bracing himself, he shouted: "Uanne, get us out of here!" He tried to plug the small leak above his head, but it was impossible. Uanne steered the shuttle into a twist, then a high G turn. She cranked it up to maximum thrust. Up became down. The rear of the shuttle accelerated toward him. Floating helplessly, Orto had time enough to scream out: "Commander!"

Then everything faded.

Chapter Four

Surprise Crisis Aftermath

Amenia: *the goddess of health and property rights, brought forward the first knowledge of Arseina's medical plants and herbs, thought to have happened in pre-T.W.C.T., year 7. During her medical travels Amenia counseled the sick and dying. Early Arseinan civilization suffered greatly from resource shortages. The goddess, Amenia, took stock of the resources slated for the sick and dying, reminding the community of its needs. If the sick were slow to recover or they died, their possessions and wealth were appraised and dispersed to new owners. Arsenia's citizens say the Amenia prayer to the sick and dying. Sometimes they will quote it to the injured, using it in a humorous vein to encourage speedy recoveries. The prayer goes: "The winds of your health may be diminishing, but the value of your possessions remains strong; recover today if you need them tomorrow." Amenia, the Resourceful.* **Guild Historical Records.**

On the shuttle they had reached their extreme limit. Tired and out of time, they raced for the scout ship's protective shields. Commander Onno watched helplessly as the ship's acceleration pressed Orto against the rear bulkhead.

"E.T.A, two minutes, Commander," Uanne said. She knew two minutes might be too late.

Commander Onno spoke into the ship-to-ship radio. "*Urisa*, have the doctor standing by. Orto appears to be unconscious."

"Roger, Commander, a medical team will be waiting at the shuttle bay."

"Stand by to raise shields as soon as we land, Onno out." Uanne pushed the shuttle past *Urisa* at full speed, as she prepared for emergency braking.

"Breaking in three, two, one," Uanne announced. She spun the shuttle's nose over its engine, reversing their positions. Inside the shuttle it felt as if they'd slammed into a wall.

As Orto flew forward, Onno grabbed him. "Hang on, buddy, doctor's on his way," Onno said barely able to keep his grip on the Chief Engineer.

As Uanne lined the shuttle up with the shuttle bay, two trap doors swung open, allowing the shuttle to rise gracefully into the ship.

As soon as the shuttle's landing struts touched the deck, its side entry doors opened, allowing emergency crews to rush in. The chief medical officer stood over Onno. The Commander was still holding Orto, unable to let him go.

"Relax, Commander, he is in good hands. I just need to make a quick scan," said the medical officer, as he took a portable palm scanner from his suit's left forearm.

"Blood pressure is stable, no broken bones. Ok, I see a pinched nerve in his neck and-- he's not going to like this when he wakes up-- he has a concussion and cranial swelling. You getting this, Doctor?"

"Yes, he's cleared for transport. Med bay one is ready."

"All hands clear the deck," said a voice over the speaker. "Medical transport is on the way from shuttle bay." Onno removed his safety harness and stepped out of the shuttle.

"Commander," Anna said softly, gently laying a hand on his chest, "what do you think you were looking at over there?"

"To tell you the truth..." Onno started, but he couldn't complete his answer.

"All hands brace for impact," said a voice from the speaker. Just then a shock wave knocked them down, Anna on top of Onno. .

As they recovered, Onno grinned, and said: "You sure you want to do this here, Captain? The crew'll record it on video, and sell it at the first port... and I'll bet they don't give us our cut."

"Come on, we need to get to the bottom of this," Anna said, pulling Onno off the floor.

Orto lay in Med Bay One, while the doctor energized the cellular regeneration field. Cellular regeneration—discovered on an estranged world in 138 T.W.C.T—brought on rapid cellular recovery and growth. It often eliminated the need for further medical intervention.

As Orto received hours of cellular regeneration, he felt a creeping awareness of something he couldn't identify, yet was very real. This grew into an atmosphere in his mind that was much like fog. Like someone wandering in the thickest of mists, Orto felt detached from time, and unable to make sense of anything. He detected no features or details of any kind—just the uniform grayness of nothing.

Then something changed. At first it was so subtle he barely noticed. Then he began to see contours of faint images. Gradually these images became more familiar. Colors brightened and borders sharpened. What he was seeing began to relate to what he thought might be there when his eyes opened. These shifting impressions played out against the one thing he clearly understood: radiating pain. As this eased a bit, his mind focused on a shape forming in front of him. Orto was staring up at his Captain, Anna Urisa.

"Uh...um, Captain?"

"Easy," she said, relieved to see him conscious.

As a new wave of pain crashed through him, Orto struggled to speak. "How did I get here?"

"We brought you here to recover," Anna said. She'd been saying the prayer taught by the goddess of recovery and health, Amenia. Now that Orto was awake, she repeated it: "The winds of your health may be diminishing, but the value of your possessions remains strong; recover today if you need them tomorrow."

Upon hearing the words, Orto remembered what happened.

"Captain..." Orto rasped. "The shuttle?"

Anna placed her hand on his chest and gave him her "mom" look. She knew the shuttle's damage reports ("...repairs will take several weeks...") were the last thing he needed. "Orto, everyone is ok, and the shuttle is parked safely on board. A little banged up, nothing that can't be fixed. Rest, my friend, and let me know if you need anything."

"Thank you, Captain. If you could...need... data, pad."

Anna —looked at him and shook her head. Here he was, barely conscious, and he wanted to study the download.

"Later," she replied. "Rest well, my friend."

As Orto slept Med Bay One pulsed with blue energy. A night nurse made her rounds, then sat down next to Orto's bay, her back against the wall. She occupied herself by monitoring Orto's medical readings. The ship's illumination system was in gray mode, simulating night. The blue glow of the cellular regeneration field was the one bright light in the darkness. Orto twitched. His nurse felt breeze brush her hair. She glanced at her data pad, then looked up. Had something moved?

Orto awoke with a start. The vision of the dead man on the lifeboat was still fresh in his mind.

"Where...where's the captain?" Orto croaked.

Surprised to see he was conscious, the nurse struggled to answer: "Uh...um, sir, this is the night shift."

"Night shift?" Orto's perceptions were confused. He wondered where he was, and why. Without thinking he began to sit up, swinging his legs over the side.

His nurse gently pushed him back into the pillows." "Little more time on the med bay, sir. You aren't ready yet."

"Captain!" Orto yelled, "Captain!" Tears slipped down his cheeks. "Captain! Captain! I need to tell the Captain!" Suddenly he grasped the nurse's collar and pulled her face toward his. "He appeared to me. He said we must leave this place."

"Ok, ok," said the nurse, gently detaching his fingers from her uniform. "First you need to let me go, and then maybe I can help."

Orto relinquished his grip. His eyes cleared, and he spoke slowly. "There was a guy... the guy Commander Onno and I were talking to earlier."

"I understand," the nurse said, activating a switch on the med bay control panel.

As the nurse kept speaking in soothing tones Orto's eyes started to close,.

"Give me a couple of minutes and I will contact the Captain," she said. Her voice was a gentle murmur. She administered a sedative without Orto even being aware of it. "You can tell her your story first thing in the morning."

Orto slept.

it was several hours later that Anna stirred in her sleep. Something about Orto touched her unconscious mind, and she awakened with a sudden need to check on him. She tossed her bed covers and activated the communications panel on the wall.

"Med Lab, this is the Captain," she said. "Is there any news on Orto?"

"Yes, Captain," said the on-duty physician, Dr. Sanguine. "He's awake, active, and he's been popping up all over the Med Lab, looking for something to do. We cleared him for light duty, giving him instructions that he's supposed to rest if he feels at all tired. Last I saw he was headed for his post, but that was hours ago. If you don't find him in Engineering, he's probably in his quarters."

"Thank you, Doctor. It's good to hear he is returning to normal."

"One last thing," said Doctor Sanguine. "He went on and on about a body he found in ship wreckage. In his head--- I guess in a dream—he saw the body, as if it were alive. He said it was telling us to leave the sector. Visions are fairly normal in recoveries like this, but he can't let go of it. Our nurse had to sedate him in order to complete the last cycle of his treatment."

"Ok," Anna said, looking at her feet. "I will—uh, see what I can learn. Captain Urisa out."

She sat, sleepy and a trifle guilty, unable to contemplate further rest. Anna felt responsible for Orto's injury. The Guild's philosophy governing scout ships went through her head, and she mumbled the words: "Mark it and move on." But a question burrowed under her thoughts: *Would we have investigated if I'd never felt compelled to look for my father?*

She reactivated the com panel, and found her Chief Engineer's settings. "Orto," she called into it.

"Orto, here, Captain."

"I heard you have been released for light duty."

"Yes, Captain. The doctor gave me a few hours before I have to return to his rest schedule."

Anna took a deep breath. "I'm happy you're back on your feet, but I'd like to see how you're doing first hand. Stop by my room."

"Yes, Captain. There was something I wanted to tell you..."

"Absolutely Tell me when you get here," Anna said, wondering if she should change out of her night clothes.

The single thought about hiding something that revealed she was a woman disturbed her. Anna liked to maintain her feminine look and feel. She waited for Orto, her hair sweeping slightly below her shoulders, to where it touched her favorite sleepwear. Her skin tingled when she thought about the silky nightgown underneath a red robe with black highlights, flaring into an almost transparent material at her hands and thighs. Anna enjoyed the simple pleasures in life, and in her sleepwear she could feel a liberating sensation, if not pleasure—as if air itself sought the gratification of touching her skin.

A chime sounded at the door.

"Captain."

"When you're here in my room, call me Anna, Orto."

"Yes, Captain, I mean Anna," Orto said.

Anna invited Orto to sit on the bed with her. "It's not going to bite. I was hoping to see how you are doing."

"I'm doing better; the nurse said I gave her a scare."

"I heard. I'm sure she'll be fine, but are you doing ok...hurting anywhere?"

"No, uh, Anna," Orto said looking away.

Anna remained silent, shifting her legs, hoping that showing a little skin would make him more comfortable.

"I am glad you invited me here, Anna," said Orto.

"I am too, Orto," Anna said smiling. "The knowledge you were hurt, it…" Anna looked away, feeling her emotions.

"It's ok, Anna," Orto said, laying his hand on her leg. Anna laid her hand on his, feeling comfort from his words.

"I know what you're thinking and I know the risk, but it's a risk worth pursuing. Besides, I think this time we are all going to benefit from the find."

"The find?" Anna said, still holding Orto's hand.

"I am going to tell you something and I need you to keep an open mind."

Anna nodded.

"Ok, where do I start?" Orto said looking around. "Have you ever been to my family's shipyard in orbit of Turanno? Whether you have or not, you should understand: Every ship made, no matter the name used in service, has a service number. No two ships have the same service number, nor are any ships following a numerical pattern. Whatever ship is created first has the preceding number. Some ships require more time than others to build. So no numerical pattern in the creation of ships, right?"

Anna kept nodding, still holding his hand.

"That's what we're trained to believe, but that ship we found here is one of twelve that were built at the same time. There are only twelve ships in Guild history, of the same class, built at the same time, at the same shipyard. I know where one is now, but until recently I thought that was the only one still in existence. The data we found is badly damaged, but I've customized a program that will recover as much of it as possible. The life pod Commander Onno and I stepped on is--or was--one of the twelve."

Orto could see Anna didn't understand.

"Anna, your dad's ship was Number Twelve. Normally, I wouldn't have thought to check these things but when I worked at the family shipyard the Guild brought in a derelict they said had been found adrift. One of my duties was to examine a ship and list the parts we could salvage and sell. Nothing in Guild space goes to waste. Walking the ship bow-to-stern, I realized there was something peculiar about the design. I couldn't build a parts manifest for it, so I called Guild central and asked for a classification and blueprints-- you need to know what ships your spare parts will fit in." Orto saw that Anna was captivated. "You know what they say, uh, wait… sorry.. you wouldn't…" Orto realized he was stumbling.

Anna pulled his hand back onto her leg, allowing him to touch her skin. His confidence returned.

"So, ok, Guild had no record or any listing of any kind. I had the ship pulled out of the decommissioning yard, and parked it. It was going to take some time to find out what we could use those parts for, but daily responsibilities and a back log of salvage operations pushed it out of my mind."

Anna listened, waiting. She kept her burning question at bay, but she had to know.

"What about my father's ship?"

"Almost there, Anna. If I don't tell the whole story, nothing will make sense. As the demand for parts grew, so did my special ability. I spent years gutting ships of the same class for parts. I knew what would function and malfunction better than anyone. Ship repair became the next phase of our business. I needed to learn faster than demand grew--not easy, especially when other companies started demanding services we weren't ready for. Installing parts and basic repair, well, that's one thing but hull repairs and guidance systems--that's a totally different set of instructions. My dad knew I could do it, so more and more was piled on me. I had to lay the ground floor for an entirely new shipyard. Gone were the days of floating around a docked ship, parts in tow, or walking the skin with magnetic boots. With our new setups I could bring in a ship, spin it around, turn it, cut it in sections, and give full instructions, without ever leaving my workstation. I would split the work as needed. Most of it was skin and frames. You know the Guild motto: 'Waste nothing.'"

Anna stopped him. "I need to know, Orto, how did you know my dad's ship was one of the twelve? I don't know what that means, do you?"

"You need to trust me; this is the best way to tell you."

"I understand," she said. "Go on."

"As chief mechanic it was my job to find the faults in older ships' guidance systems," Orto went on. "Let me tell you, it wasn't easy until I started checking other ship systems. Computers are only as good as the program running them, so I started rewriting software for the older computers. They needed cleaner lines of code governing their operations. To do this I needed to back up the computer's memory.

"Not every ship's captain wanted to let me download from their computer memories. I often ran into encrypted operating protocols for key ship systems. The source was usually the same: alterations in the base line code. People tweaked systems their way, and wanted to keep their methods secret. Knowledge gives an advantage. But our job out here is to find valuable resources, or technology, and leaked information tends to undermine claims. So I did what any self-respecting tech would do: I cracked their encryption and downloaded everything. Once I had it, I fixed their mess with a streamlined program, the re-encrypted their files before sending them on their way. They never knew the difference. It was around that time that I recalled the ship wallowing in the decommissioning bays. The thought of it game me an idea. Even when a computer's core memory is erased, some trace data lingers. Almost anything that's been there might be recoverable. I tried it.

"That ship became my ship--a pet project. I spent all my free time on its restoration. As I told you earlier, it's a museum piece now, but that is not why I'm telling this story. What I'm about to say is something the Guild still wants hidden: I learned from the captain's log that the twelve ships were commissioned to do a specific job: an origins search."

Anna stopped him. "Origins... my father once told me our gods hadn't originated in Arseina, I never gave it much thought."

Orto resumed his story: "Until now I was never able to find a parts manifest, or engineering details, for my ship. It's hard to hide something you might need right away, so it wasn't hidden. The crewman we found over there was the chief engineer. He left a personal recording, full of data. It's explosive stuff, Anna. I recommend we keep this quiet. If the Guild knows we found it, they may strip you of your authority as captain." Anna's eyes lit up.

"What... why?"

"They worked hard to hide the identity of the twelve ships: the one I had, this ship we just found, your father's ship, and the rest. I found the parts list and engineering documents listing twelve ships with high capacity engines. Today the design is commonplace, but when these ships came off the line they could out-fly and out-run any ship built at that time. It could even give today's ships a run for their money. But the ship we had benefitted from my modifications." Orto was obviously proud of his work.

Anna pulled away, and lay back, unconcerned about modesty.

"You think my father might have been involved in some kind of secret origins search?"

"I don't know, but it's starting to point in that direction. Do you feel up to an investigation?"

"Is that possible?" she asked.

Orto shrugged. "Yes, though there's a lot of corruption in the data we recovered."

"Orto," Anna said softly, "I am sorry if this is a challenging question, but when I talked to the doctor he said you scared the nurse about a dream."

"Yes, I remember," he said, shaking his head and looking at the floor.

"It was something, a dream you could call it. I don't even know. Real... it felt real." Orto paused then turned to Anna.

"Have you ever remembered something from your past, something that stayed with you? A memory so vivid that it comes to life? What I saw was a dream, yet it was alive and I could see it. I know it wasn't real but it was...looking at it now, my memory I think is intact. Onno and I encountered the crewman. He never stood up nor was he alive, I clearly remember that. Yet he was somehow animated. I clearly remember that too. In the dream he floated just off the floor, and when I knelt down to recharge his suit he grabbed my arm and faced me. I can still hear his words."

"What did he say?" Anna asked.
"He said: 'Leave now! Only death awaits you!'"
Anna had no response. It was rest time for Orto.

Chapter Five

Out of Frying Pan—Into Fire

To all Guild Scout Ships: when on assignment it is the right of all Guild Captains to determine mission protocols when determining course and destination. The Guild authorizes, at captain's discretion, the abdication of mission objectives, when evidence or crew opinion suggest plotting a jump to any system, uncharted or not, holds greater potential for, wealth, resources, technology, or anything of value.

Guild Directive, Number 8

As alarms sounded throughout the ship, Anna slammed her fist down, activating the inter-ship communications.

"Command Deck, report," she snapped.

"Captain, a ship just appeared, unknown configuration, - bearing down on our position." Commander Onno reported.

Anna stared at Orto, then leapt from her bed. "Tell me the rest later. Get down to engineering and stand by. Still in her night clothes, she sprinted out to the corridor, calling out orders: "Command Deck, activate defensive batteries and stand by. I'm on my way."

"Captain, glad you're here," Onno said, noticing her lack of uniform.

"Ship, unknown configuration, bearing down on our position," Uanne said.

"Raise shields. Plot a jump, Uanne, and stand by."

"Roger, Captain," Uanne said, pulling up star charts. It seemed as if uncharted space stretched in every direction.

"Make sure you give us some distance; neighboring systems may not be friendly."

"Roger, Captain, plotting course," said Uanne, uncertain if a clean jump was possible. Uncharted jumps required short bursts, as well as time to measure distance and obstructions. A second alarm blared. Anna activated ship-wide communications, "All hands brace for impact… Helm bow thirty degrees down angle, speed three-quarters sub-light, Commander."

"Yes, Captain."

"Defensive batteries one-through-five, rake his belly when…"

Suddenly a muffled thud and explosion shook the ship.

"Report!"

"Their first shot glanced off our hull," Onno said, feeling a small bit of relief.

Anna returned to ship-wide communications: "All departments prepare for decompression." She turned to Onno. "They're firing kinetic sabot rounds. Load batteries five-through-ten, sabots."

"Roger, Captain, coming into range—all batteries report ready."

"Thank you, Commander, Fire!" Anna said.

Defensive batteries rose from their ports. Flashes of charged energy hit enemy craft as they passed under.

"Report," Anna said.

"Minimal impact; shields holding," Onno barked.

"Sabots now," Anna ordered.

High-speed sabot rounds designed to penetrate armored hulls blasted from the batteries, piercing layers of the ship, as they compressed the atmosphere past survivable tolerances.

"Helm, down angle ninety degrees, port side turn forty-five. Let's see if we can break his firing solution," Anna said. A massive hit ripped through several decks. It was followed by another.

Decompression alarms sounded throughout the ship. Onno turned and faced the Captain. "We won't survive a second round like that. We have to jump the ship."

"Agreed," Anna said. "Uanne, jump the ship."

"Yes, Captain," Uanne began uploading jump coordinates.

As new alarms sounded, Uanne inserted her jump key into the navigation command station. She waited for the board to flash green and turned the key.

Bristling with power, Guild ship *Urisa* surged forward into a vortex of bright blue energy. All outside contact ceased. Communications went silent. Midway Station 14, and all visible stars disappeared, replaced by a blue haze. Anna realized she's lost all contact with the Guild. Her present concern was more immediate: repair.

"Commander, Orto is going to need the help. Go below and oversee the work."

"Yes, Captain."

"Wait, Commander Onno, one last thing," she said. "Was there any communication from us or them?"

"No, said the Commander. "We tried repeatedly on all channels. It's all we could do."

"Rodger. Give me a report as soon as you can." Anna signed off, troubled by the whole business.

The ship moved gracefully, restoring the feeling of life. Anna liked the feel pulsating from the ship's jump drive. She sat in her command chair with her eyes closed, enjoying the moment. The com panel, chimed for her attention.

"Captain here, go ahead."

"Captain, Commander Onno reporting. Damage is extensive but manageable. A third of the ship is uninhabitable, including...." Onno paused with discomfort, "your room."

"What?" Anna said, shocked.

"Sorry, Captain, but that's not the worst news. First round penetrated three decks and made its way back out into space before we jumped. The second is still lodged near engineering. Someone said they thought they saw something coming out of it but that hasn't been confirmed."

"Ok, just give me a time frame for repairs."

"One, maybe two, planetary rotations before vented areas of the ship can be pressurized. I'm sorry, Captain. One positive note, many of the crewmen were happy to see you in only your nightgown."

Anna laughed. "Perhaps we should have a sleepwear party when this is over. I believe some ancient civilization called them 'sleepovers'."

"Sounds good, Captain. Commander Onno, out." The temperature on the command deck dropped several degrees Anna huddled in her command chair. Lights started to flicker.

"Captain," Uanne called out.

"Stand by, Uanne, I saw it too. Captain Urisa to engineering."

"Onno here, Captain."

"Onno, where's Orto?"

"He was stabilizing the reactor, but left to hand out instructions for work crews. Wait...."

Orto's chief deputy spoke up: "Sorry, Captain. He was last seen chasing down power disruptions. Did you need to talk to him?"

"No, that's ok—looks like he is aware of everything. Our lights started flickering up here; I thought he should know."

"Understood. We're getting multiple reports like that."

"Roger, Commander. Let's keep this channel open so I can hear what's going on." Anna scanned every station on the command deck. Everything from Navigation to Helm Control Security was operated by skilled crewmembers. Auxiliary stations, like Engineering, Survey, or the mapping stations were active but on standby. Anna pulled her legs in closer. Cooler air mixed with insecurity, giving her tingles. The hair on her arms stood straight up. "Ah, um, I just got the chills," said Anna. She jumped to her feet.

On her home planet, moving around was the solution during periods of extreme cold; the chill was hard to fight once it settled in. The body's ability to overcome the cold was good, but sometimes life's only answer was aggressive movement. Still barefoot, Anna strutted around the command deck, enduring the cold steel touching the soles of her feet. She had no choice. Keep moving and stimulate blood flow or huddle and hope the cold air wouldn't numb the mind. Anna stopped. She saw that stations in standby were losing power.

"Onno," Anna call out, "we're losing power up here."

"Stand by, Captain," Onno said hurriedly.

Stressed voices cracked from the command deck's com channel, giving situation reports. Anna felt something was missing.

"Captain," Uanne cried, "jump drive is failing.".

Guild ship *Urisa*, bristling with power, streaming through a vortex of bright energy, was suddenly breaking down. There were uncontrolled surges in the jump drive. Uanne monitored the navigation computer just beneath her feet. Theirs was the only station using Guild backup power. The ship shook violently, knocking down Anna. Every station on the command deck went dark.

"My station is working on emergency power only, Captain," Uanne reported. "Jump drive is down, entering normal space." Anna scrambled up to Uanne. Everything on the command deck was dark including lights. Only a few lights were tied into the emergency power below them.

"Pull up a navigation scan of the area; we're landing," Anna said, accepting the danger. As the ship hurtled into the unknown, Uanne glanced at the navigation readout.

"We are inside a star system," she breathed. "Large space body, no atmosphere, directly in our flight path…. Captain, it's a moon orbiting a planet with a breathable atmosphere!"

"Onno, you getting …" Anna started.

"Sorry, Captain," Uanne interrupted. "This planet's inhabited radio and atomic readings are off the charts."

Anna hesitated.

"Captain," Onno called from his spot on the Command Deck, "Orto has tied in enough emergency power for landing thrusters only. Antigravity generator is off line. That moon is our best chance of landing in one piece."

Anna waited, hoping he would see some other choice. When silence reigned, she said: "Ok, land the ship, Uanne." She went to Onno. "What's going on here?" she murmured, embracing her friend.

"I'm afraid there's more bad news," he said. "We'll have to abandon ship."

"What? "Abandon the newest star of the Guild fleet?" She pushed Onno away.

"We might have a chance to come back but not now. Orto just left for the shuttle pod."

"That's not safe to fly."

"I know. Hear me out. As soon as we land he'll decompress the entire ship. There must have been something in that Sabot round lodged in the bulkhead. It chases down power distribution units; we've never seen anything like it. It...it...seems to be alive, consuming anything with a high concentration of energy, growing stronger every time."

Anna couldn't believe what she was hearing—a monster in her ship eating its way through the energy conduits.

"Preposterous," she said, not knowing who should be the target of that word.

"Uanne," Onno insisted, "land the ship and join me and the Captain in the Command Deck's escape pod. Whatever it is, it's still feasting on power from the main reactor. We have a short window of survival."

"Roger, Commander, loading auto landing instructions now," Uanne said.

Alarms sounded throughout the ship, Orto announced: "Shipwide decompression under way. Get to your escape pods."

Onno assisted Anna into her seat on the pod. Uanne took up her customary navigation duty post, while Onno buckled in and sealed the hatch.

"Commander Onno to all escape pods: Clear the ship, establish stable orbit, and wait for further instructions." Confirmations came in from all pods.

"Take us out, Lieutenant," Anna said. The escape pod shot out from the ship long before landing instructions took over. After establishing stable orbit, Uanne spun the escape pod around.

"I don't need to watch, Uanne," Anna said, squeezing her eyes shut. She felt as if she were abandoning an essential part of herself.

Onno activated the escape pod's communications.

"Orto," Onno said wearily, "activate the distress signal."

"Roger, Commander. Activation under way," Orto paused for a moment searching for the right words. "Commander, I recommend we put some space between us and the ship. Communications between escape pods may, how should I say, become unusable. Venting the ship will hopefully stop further damage, but without any form of solid assurance, I moved the emergency deep space transmitter into the shuttle pod and cranked up the transmitter's power. It won't last very long but it will strengthen our chance of overcoming the two-light-year limit."

Anna listened, drawing up a plan. "Orto, can this planet pick up our message?"

"Stand by, Captain," Orto said, taking the time to study the signal strength and modulations. "Judging by what I am reading that is a very strong possibility."

"Orto," Anna called out. "Orto!"

She could hear him gasping. Finally he spoke: "Captain... you are not going to believe this. Some of the communications down there are videoing multiple sources emanating across large continuants." He paused to check something. "Captain, directing video feed over to you; tell me what you see."

Anna watched something she barely understood and turned to Uanne with a touch of suspicion.

"Uanne," the Captain said with a look of discomfort, "did you know anything about this world? And are you under any Guild instructions, commands or requests?"

"Captain?"

Anna directed the video to everyone's station. She saw their shocked reactions.

"Captain, they....they are us!" Uanne cried.

Beings who looked exactly like their long-dead ancestors played on the video feeds. This wasn't recordings of past events. It was happening in real time.

Captain Anna Urisa made the final call to land. "Our situation is grave. We've come to a place where Guild law can only be looked at as a set of guidelines. Keep the faith, and remember the words of the Guild father, Lanay Achurem: 'The only time we fail is when we stop looking for opportunities.'"

Chapter Six

Message in a Bottle

Dr. Robert Guttenberg drank the last of his scotch, and slammed the glass onto the table. He, eyed a month-old copy of the Sun Times. His nightly ritual entailed a glass of scotch and a look at the front page. Today's was dated June 15, 1958.

He glanced at the front page photo, reading the caption: "National Aeronautics Research Consortium (NARC), opens its headquarters in Maine. Director Robert J. Guttenberg, presides over ceremony." Robert had gotten used to the title of Doctor over the last thirteen years, but now, with the Doctor's forty-first birthday just past, America's President Andrew Summers had laid the burden of the National Aeronautics Research Consortium on his shoulders. It was all because of Sputnik.

A shadow of fear lingered in his mind every time he looked at that newspaper. He needed all the courage he could muster, including that in a bottle. Once the whiskey had washed away his fear he stumbled off to bed.

He'd crossed over into sleep when the phone started ringing. He groped blindly in the darkness, finding only his nightstand. His hand struck something. Pain shot through him. He saw the radium-painted numbers glowing on the clock. " "03:30 hours! You've got to be kidding. This better be good!" He found the phone. "Hello," he growled sleepily.

"Robert!" It was the lovely Doctor Sing. "You need to get down here; you won't believe what is happening."

"What…you know what time it is?"

"Yes, but, wake up, Robert. That signal is not a Soviet satellite. Contact, Robert! We have Contact!"

He came fully awake, "You what? Ok. I will be there; give me a few minutes to throw on some clothes." He laid the down the receiver. Was this real? Sleep had a deceptive way of telling a story. But he was sure he was conscious. They'd been tracking a Soviet probe that had crashed on the moon. That had seemed like the mission for the month, but this was different. Something this big would guarantee the lab's funding for years to come. "Why can't these things happen in the damn daytime," Robert wondered as he stubbed his toe. "That's not too much to ask, is it?"

On any other morning it wouldn't have been a long drive to the lab, but today his red 1948 Mercury cut the time almost in half. With all four wheels locking, the car lurched into Robert's favorite parking spot just outside his office window. "Damn!" he said, slamming his car door. "Few more feet and I could have parked in my office."

Guttenberg was one of those people who could never go fast enough. He walked fast, drove fast, and preferred to work fast. Robert looked at his watch again. *04:06... moving too slow.* He rushed to his office.

In his office he slipped on his lab coat, then went out into the hallway. As he accelerated past several labs, he tried to button his lab coat. He didn't notice when he mismatched the buttons and holes. The one thing he did notice was silence. "Holy smokes... where is everybody? 'Contact.' What the hell does it mean?"

A flight of stairs at the end of the hallway led to another flight descending below ground several hundred feet. Robert entered into an area of the complex affectionately called *the Silo*. The complex was set up like a wagon wheel, with stairs and elevators to the surface in the outer ring. Like spokes of a wagon wheel, tunnels ran three hundred yards, meeting at the center of the underground complex. There they emptied into a cavern bigger than the Silo. Robert had only been down here once. He emerged from the tunnel, and stepped into the cavern. In the center was a perfectly round hole descending a hundred feet and measuring two hundred yards across. Robert continued his descent, almost reaching the floor. Centralized computer control stations circled just above him. Looking up, he realized that it did look like a silo. It rose above the cavern, cutting a path to the surface equal in width to the carved out hole in the bottom. Yellow painted barriers circled the facility, preventing man or machines from falling to the bottom of the silo. Workstations formed a crescent far above his head, allowing the barrier to form a back stop for the equipment. The lower floor was set up like a maze, with computers, cords, data, terminals and data storage devices crowded everywhere.

Robert finally found the research team gathered around a central control station.

"I am not sure what to make of it," said one of the scientists examining the control station readings. "Nothing in the world could produce a signal this strong and this complicated. My god, man, look at this printout. You know what this means, it means... well, I am not sure what it means but we need to know more."

An attractive woman poked her head up from behind the workstation, and saw Robert coming. "Good morning, sunshine," she said with a touch of sarcasm. "I am so pleased you could join us."

"I'm sorry, what was your name again?"

She looked at Guttenberg and narrowed her eyes. "Sing Ann Howell...Director Sing Ann Howell." Laughter burst from the other scientists. Dr. Howell approached Guttenberg, and ran her finger down the lapel of his lab coat, giving him a friendly smile, "Be a gentlemen, Robert, and offer a woman a cigarette."

Howell watched his embarrassment grow. She was new to the lab, with her first Ph.D. in Mathematics from Tokyo University and second in Computer Engineering from Harvard. A product of Japan's postwar reconstruction process, Robert felt she was the wave of the future, and she was cute.

As Guttenberg pulled out a cigarette, Sing prolonged his discomfort by pulling two pins from her hair, letting it spill to her shoulders. She took the cigarette, then turned to the men behind her. "One of you boys have a light?" A handful of Zippo lighters appeared. She chose one, then took a long drag. She crossed her arms, eyed Guttenberg, and asked, "So what would you like to know?"

"I would like to know— wait, what are you doing?"

Dr. Howell put the cigarette between her lips, then reached up and unbuttoned his lab coat. "Hold still, honey, I will tell you everything you need to know, but first I need to get you dressed properly." She corrected his fiasco with the buttons.

"I was under the impression it was important," said Guttenberg.

"It is."

"So what is it?"

"A signal."

"A signal--so what?"

"Not just any signal."

Robert rolled his eyes. "Ok, I'll play."

"It's big."

"How big?"

"So big we're having trouble keeping up with it."

"Explain."

Dr. Howell showed Robert the image on the oscilloscope. "It's the data rate-- more data in the signal than our computers can handle. We've switched to recording the signal with the hope that we can process it later. We might be able to compress it into a data burst, but we won't know until we start processing."

"Where's the message coming from?"

"The moon."

"The moon?"

"Yes, the moon."

"Who could be transmitting from the moon?"

"It's not the Russians or the United States."

"How can you tell?"

"It's simple. Contrary to what you've been telling yourself, size really does matter."

Guttenberg's eyes got really big, he took a breath but it was too late. All the air in the room was gone.

She drew close and said in a whispered voice, "This is no earthly signal."

"I am almost afraid to ask how you know?" said Robert.

"It's digital."

"That's it... it's digital?"

"Yep."

"So? We've been transmitting in digital for years."

"Not like this."

"Ok, explain."

"It's simple, in my country we have a saying *you can't pack twenty pounds of rice in a five pound bag.* We are at capacity trying to receive this message, everything in the country is pointed toward the moon and it's taking multiple stations to pipe everything down here. We're at recording capacity. I've been making calls all night trying to get enough data storage lined up to record the whole message. It's like we're driving a Model T and they're coming at me in a supersonic jet—only it's a thousand times stranger. Processing this signal may take months... even years."

"Have we recorded the message in its entirety?"

"We think so. Fortunately for us, it repeats thirty seconds after the last transmission."

"Every thirty seconds, how long is the message?"

"Two minutes, give or take a few seconds," she said.

Doctor Guttenberg's hands shook as he tried to light a cigarette.

"Here, let me," said Dr. Howell flipping open her Zippo.

"Wait a minute. I thought you didn't have a lighter."

Howell shrugged her shoulders, "Careful about making false assumptions. I just asked if anyone had a light."

Puffing on his cigarette, Doctor Guttenberg stepped back, noting all the new equipment. Its distinctive hum filled his ears; enough power to power a small city. The computers and electrical gear ate energy, and produced a huge amount of heat. They were all hard at work this morning.

"Good thing they put all these computers deep underground," he said, glancing around.

"Natural convection, doctor."

"What?"

"Cooling by natural convection," she said. "You remember, warm air rising and cool air settling. The warm air naturally rises to the top of the silo, cooling on its way up due to the natural heat dissipation of the surrounding earth."

Robert grimly nodded. This method of air conditioning almost eliminated the need for standard cooling units when running power hungry computers. "All this and it's not enough," he said. "A simple hello could blow out every transistor and electrical part invented to date." He extinguished his cigarette and paused to pull his thoughts together.

"Oh, come now, it's not that bad. A little challenging, yes, but it shows us where we need to focus our industrial and engineering talents for the next ten or...forty years," Dr. Howell said, wrapping her arm around his. "I'll walk you back to the surface, Robert. I am sure you will need to make a few phone calls when we get back to your office." She paused. "And, Robert, call me Sing. I have a feeling we will be working together for quite awhile."

The time on the wall clock read 05:30. Doctor Guttenberg sat staring at his phone.

"Staring at it won't help you make that call," Sing said, sitting on the opposite side of the desk.

"I know, I know...I'm just thinking about what I need to say."

"'Hello, I need to talk to President Summers' would be a good start. I think the rest will take care of itself." Sing winked at Robert, then sat up in her chair and grabbed the phone. "If you want I can make the call for you."

"Hey, put that down, I'll call. After all, it's not *your* career on the line here."

"I would think your precious career would be in more trouble if you wait. Some other government agency might make that call."

"Good point. Ok, here goes." He dialed. When he heard a woman answer, he said: "Oh, um, Peggy, this is Director Guttenberg. I need—I am doing fine, how are you? I—yes, need to make a call, that's right. The White House--use the direct line they gave us a few weeks ago... Ok, I will." Guttenberg covered the phone with his hand, and whispered across his desk, "I'm on hold."

Sing smiled and gave him a thumbs-up.

"You have the White House? Thanks, Peggy, 'Hello, yes this is Director of NARC, Doctor Robert Guttenberg. What? Yes, I can hold... Hello, I need to talk to—My name, Doctor Robert Guttenberg, Director of the NARC, I need to talk to—is it important...yes, its important! I have a priority message for the President. What...? No, I can't tell you, it's for the Pres—ok...it's about time, I will hold. Mr. President, what do I have for you...? A message... What's the message? That's just it, we received a message, I understand your time is limited... the message? The message, we received a mess—what? I am telling you the message, we received a signal from the far side of the moon. That's right...I don't know how it got there. I needed to inform you the signal is not from Earth...I know I just told you it's from the moon... Yes, that's right, I don't know who it's from...but it's not from anyone on this Earth. The message didn't say anything. At least we don't know what is in the mess—I don't know who the message is for. We received the signal at 03:30 hours this—yes... we have a copy. It's big—huge—that's why we believe it's not manmade. It repeats every thirty seconds. It's taken every storage device we have to record what we think is a two-minute message. No...we haven't started processing. It's taken every computer we have just to record it... Yes sir, I understand, sir, around the clock—ok, I will give the word to everyone and redouble our efforts, Thank you for your time, Mr. President, and goodbye."

As he hung up, Doctor Guttenberg looked sheepishly at Howell, "Well, get ready to call this place home for a while, Sing. We're not going anywhere for a very long time. Round the clock shifts, starting tonight."

Dr. Howell smiled, "That's ok, Robert, I don't like sleeping alone anyway."

"You may change that tune in a few days. We have a supply of cots in the storage locker. I think it's time to pull some of them out. I think we'll need them all.

Chapter Seven

Robert's Paradox

Robert watched another sunset from his office window. Nearly a week had gone by with little to show. Many of the staff hadn't slept in several days; judging by the smell, some hadn't showered either. The work was uppermost on his mind when he heard a familiar voice down the hall. He knew what was coming. He rubbed his eyes, recalling the bottle of scotch in his desk. The thought of the shadowy, sexy Sing prancing into his office left him longing for a drink. A large frosted window made up the top half of his office door. He saw her outline through the glass, then the door opened.

"Hey, I thought I would find you hiding in here," said Sing.

"I am not hiding... I'm... thinking."

"Call it what you want, your secret is safe with me. What were you thinking about, anyway?"

"Getting a drink. Interested?" Guttenberg asked.

"My place or yours," she replied.

Guttenberg sat up quickly. "You serious?"

"Are you?" Sing said without skipping a beat. "We both really need to get out of here for a while and I don't care where it is. Clean clothes and a fresh shower and a couple of drinks and I will be out like a light. I'm too tired to drive so you can take me to my place or I can sleep on your couch. I just need to get out of here."

"Come to think of it, this place is starting to feel like the morning after a wild frat party. Just a second," Robert said, picking up the phone. "NARC switchboard, this is Director...oh hello, Peggy."

"Director Guttenberg, how may I help you at this late hour?"

"Peggy, by the sound of your voice I realize everyone is extremely tired, including you. I want you to call all departments and tell them to shut everything down. It's time to go home. Oh, and Peggy, call the cleaning crew, would you? Things have gotten out of hand around here."

"Certainly, sir, everyone is going to be happy to take the night off and I will send in the cleaning crew."

"Great, thanks. See you tomorrow, Peggy." He hung up and looked at Sing. "Well, that takes care of that. You ready?"

"Take the helm, Captain, our ship awaits," said Sing. "What is our course and destination?"

"You really are leaving it up to me. Well... in that case, climb onboard the Red Mercury. The ship's headed to my house. If the decision is mine, I'll vote to keep my house freshly stocked with attractive women every time. You sure you want to go there?"

"How else am I going to get that free drink you promised?"

The two headed out to the parking lot where many cars were already pulling out.

"They're not wasting any time; you would think they haven't been home for a while," Robert observed.

Sing's mind was drifting. "It is nice out tonight," she said. "Robert, did you ever think the stars could rule our future. If we have what we think we have, everything's going to change."

Robert grunted. "Be careful with your assumptions. Even If we learn the solution, it will never see the light of day. Anything we learn will be top secret for the rest of our lives. I'm certain of it." He gave the sky a sad look, then opened the passenger door for Sing.

"Get in. There's a bottle of scotch waiting for us. Nothing more we can do but get some rest." Robert took his time driving home. After all, every rare minute spent with a beautiful woman was better than one without.

When the car came to a stop, Sing looked over at him. "What does the 'J' stand for in your name?"

"If we're going to be good friends I'll tell you, but how do you know my middle initial?"

"Your mailbox, silly," she said.

"I'll tell you all about it, but first one of us needs a bath."

"Yeah and quick…" Sing trailed off until she entered Robert's house. There she looked around, and said: "Nicely done, Robert. Nicely done. I can see being director has been good to you."

"It's allowed me to furnish my house the way I always wanted to, that's for sure," he said as he started mixing drinks.

Standing on a bearskin rug in the middle of the living room, Sing removed her shoes. "Oh…oh, that's nice. Just what tired feet need." She sat down on a dark leather couch and started rubbing her feet on the rug.

Robert watched Sing lose herself in simple pleasures. "If you like that, try out that blanket on the back of the couch," he suggested.

She reached back and found a mink fur blanket, "Robert! This is simply delightful; where did you get it?"

"Here take this, and I'll tell you." As Robert handed her the promised drink, he sank into his favorite chair, a dark leather piece facing the couch. He took a long sip from his glass. "I got that from my grandfather."

"What?"

"You wanted to know where the mink blanket came from."

"Oh, yeah, tell me more."

"Ok, if I do you need to tell me something about yourself. Deal?"

"Deal, go on."

"Grandfather was a fur trader; sold furs all over the world. That's where I got my middle name: Jacob. Jacob Guttenberg owned a successful import-export business. He gave me my first job; I worked there until the War. I was slaving my way through college when the war department asked me and some other students to work on a special project. My grandfather gave me that blanket as a graduation gift when I earned my Ph.D. Small look into my life story. Not too interesting, if you ask me. How about you? I know you grew up in Japan, graduated university there and made it all the way over here, no small task given the state of the Japanese economy a few years ago."

"You're right; things were a mess. But, fortunately for me, I worked at a bar catering to American diplomats and high-ranking military officers. I made enough to pay my way through college. Harvard had an exchange program available to graduates. It didn't hurt that the president of Harvard came rolling through our bar about the same time. It wasn't really a bar--more of a nightclub. I served drinks and entertained, if you know what I mean. A few drinks, a song, and a dance, and here I am. It was that or live a life working as a pin cushion. Graduating with a Ph.D. in Mathematics really earned me nothing. That's how it was in those first years after the War. I had the best scores of my class, but even the males had a hard time finding work. Women had little hope."

"Well, Sing, I'm glad you are here. You've become a real asset to the lab."

Sing swallowed another drink. "Where's your bath, Robert? I'm ready for a long soak."

"Sure, yeah... let me show you." He led her deeper into the house, pointing out the bathroom, towels and soap. Robert turned to leave but before he could close the door, Sing spoke up.

"Don't go too far. Be a gentleman, would you, I have some laundry you need to wash."

"Sure. Fixing something to eat and making a fire are also on my list."

"If it's not too much trouble. Besides, you said it yourself. You like having a woman in your house."

"Apparently it comes with a price. Anything else?"

"I'll let you know," she said, handing him a pile of clothes. "Come to think of it, bring that blanket over here. I plan on wrapping myself in it when I'm through here."

Robert stood, somewhat startled, holding her clothes.

"What's the matter, Doctor, never seen a girl naked before?"

"I'm not that kind of doctor. And, no, I haven't seen a girl naked before, at least not quite like you, that's for sure. You are a strange cat, you know that? I'd like to think it's the alcohol going to your head. Whatever it is I'm not complaining."

"Robert."

"Yes."

"A week of running on only cat naps has really left me drained. Not sure if I could have made it another day."

"Enjoy your bath, Sing." Robert walked away, sleep overtaking him. He kept himself awake to wash their clothes , and make things ready for the following day. When he returned, the warm glow from the fireplace was the only source of illumination. It was back lighting for Sing, lying on the couch fast asleep, wearing nothing but a mink blanket. Robert could see most of her full feminine form. "You really are beautiful," he whispered. Walking back to his bedroom he wondered if it was all just a dream. Would he wake up and find out she was never there?

"I need to stop drinking," he mumbled into his pillow just before falling asleep.

"Wake up, sunshine, wake up, come on wake up," a soft female voice kept saying. As he came to, he thought he had dreamed of Sing. Lying comfortably in his bed the decision to open his eyes was made for him.

"What, who... Are? Never mind. Why are you holding my eyelids open?"

"You needed to wake up. Apparently it worked." Sing stood next to the bed, fully dressed. "Coffee is ready when you are."

"Coffee... oh, oh sure thank you. Give me a few minutes." Waving her out of his room, he lay in his bed gathering his thoughts. Doubt crept into his dazed mind. "This is so out of character...this sort of thing just doesn't happen. It's just a dream, I think." Setting the issue aside for a while, he focused on getting dressed and ready for work.

The smell of freshly brewed coffee made its way from the kitchen, provoking an immediate response. The prospect of coffee seemed to offer an escape from sluggishness and confusion. It took him several minutes just to pull on his pants. He grabbed a shirt and threw it on. Sing was waiting for him.

"Look who decided to show up. Oh...look at you. Come here, sleepy head." Sing stepped up and fixed Robert's shirt. "What is it with you and buttons, hold still will you? When I'm done I'll pour you that cup of coffee. One more, ok....done." She slapped her hand on his chest just before stepping back to grab a stainless steel pot that just finished percolating. "Cream or sugar, Robert?"

"Just black," he said with a foolish grin.

With two cups in hand, Sing sat down next to Robert at his kitchen table.

"Sure is nice to have a woman in the house," he said, enjoying his coffee.

"Don't get used to it, pal. You see a girl naked once and you think you own her," she said with a little smile.

"About that, you know I woke up this morning thinking it was all just a dream."

"You did have a dream and I was your dream come true," she said, finishing her coffee and standing up. "You are awake now, so it's time to go back to work."

Sing put her cup down and walked outside, "C'mon Robert, the car won't start itself."

Robert sat there for a few more seconds. "What is she doing to me?" he wondered.

Chapter Eight

Atlantis Rising

After a full night off, the NARC research complex slowly came back to life. Though Doctors Howell and Guttenberg got there a minute early, only a third of the staff arrived on time.

"It's good to know we're not late," Guttenberg said.

"You are judging our arrival by what standard?"

"Simple. We're not the last ones to show up."

"That's good to know. I'll use that next time I'm late," Sing said with a satisfied look. She opened the car door and headed for the rear entrance. "Come along, Robert, we don't want to be late for the meeting."

Inside, they headed straight for the conference room. The building's interior appeared as empty as the exterior.

"It looks like we have a little time on our hands," Robert remarked.

"Not a problem. If you'll call Peggy and have some pastries sent over, I'll get this coffeemaker going. Everyone's having a hard time moving this morning. Maybe coffee and something tasty will get their brain cells working."

"Good point, I'm glad you're here. I'm sure it will be another long week. I'll talk to Peggy and see if we can get some regular meals sent in on a schedule. Be back in a sec."

Sing watched Robert go, not sure if she was ready to get started herself.

Though life in the lab was still far from normal, tired faces brightened at the sight of coffee and the abundance of pastries. Director Guttenberg thought a few words would help things get started.

"Welcome back, everyone--it's been a long week. I know that one night off isn't enough, but extraordinary circumstances require extraordinary responses. It's been one week. What do we have, Dr. Howell?"

"Good morning, everyone, I hope you are ready this morning. I want to thank NARC for the pastries and coffee." After hearing a few grunts of satisfaction, she raised her cup. "And I want to thank Director Guttenberg for a little time off." After a nod from Robert, she went on: "I want to recap our efforts so far. What we do know is that the signal is definitely digital. We're still processing and, within a day or two, we hope to have at least five percent of the entire message run through our computers."

Doctor Guttenberg spoke up. "Well, our computers haven't caught fire under the strain, so we have that going for us, right?" He looked around, realizing his attempt at humor had fallen flat. He cleared his throat. "That's it, five percent. At this rate it's going to be months or even years, even if the equipment holds up."

"That's right," said Dr. Howell. "At the rate we're pushing the computers we'll start running into mechanical and electrical problems more frequently, slowing our progress even further. "I understand our backs are against the wall. They have been since day one. Ideas anyone?"

They all sat quietly, smoking, eating pastries or drinking coffee, feigning deep thought.

Dr. Howell rolled her eyes. "Am I the only one that knows what we need to do?"

"Apparently," Robert said, "what is it?"

"It's simple, we need a good hard look at whatever is sending that signal. One simple clue outside this room *might*-- and I do want to emphasize *might*-- give us a way to uncork this bottle. If we get lucky, there might be a message."

"Like what? 'Surrender your earth women'?" said one staffer.

"You have something to add Mister...." Guttenberg eyed the young man.

"Doctor Sum, Math department and yes, now that I think about it. Joking aside we need to find out what's in this message as fast as we can. It could be as simple as,' Hi, we're your intergalactic neighbors and, oh, by the way, you don't mind if a few million of us come to visit, do you?' But I think, no matter what it says, it's more complicated than that. Looking at the digital layout there's a good chance we're looking at a compressed message."

Howell's eyes flashed. "Why do you say that?"

"A look at normal digital two-way communication will show repetitive patterns in whatever signals it has," said Sum. "After processing five percent, repetitive patterns aren't showing."

"Meaning what?" Director Guttenberg said quickly.

"Meaning it could be compressed. If it's compressed we face the challenge of finding the right decompression algorithms. We may get lucky and find a key embedded in the damn thing, but the fact that we've only processed five percent tells me it may be a long time before we can test this theory... and keep in mind, it's only a theory."

Director Guttenberg scratched his chin. "We really haven't made any progress, have we?"

"No, we haven't," said Sing. "One more problem, Director."

"What is it, Dr. Howell?"

"Even if we decompress, or process the entire signal, our computers may not be able to run the program. It may simply be too large. And it may be in an alien language. If so, it could take years to figure it out, if that's at all possible. We need to find the signal's source. It may provide clues we can use down here to change our equipment and write new programs based on what we find."

"Ok, anyone else? Anyone..." Robert looked around the room. "No? Ok, back to work. If you have anything let me know."

After the last staffer shuffled out, Robert sat, feet on the conference table, as he finished a cigarette. He felt calmness wash over him. He was ready to think. He wondered what to tell the President. It was a difficult question. Only a large plate of doughnuts stopped his thoughts. "I don't know if this was the best idea," he muttered as he tried to brush the powered sugar from his pants. "Another week of this and I won't be able to stop eating these damn things."

"True," Sing said, still standing in the doorway. "Gluttony is not the solution to your problems."

"What... why are... I thought you had something to do."

"I'm doing it. I came back for some yummy doughnuts. But with all that powdered sugar all over your pants, I can see you need some help."

"You've helped me quite enough. What do you need?"

"Well... Someone's a little moody today."

"You would be too if you had to tell the President we need to invest millions of dollars, with the likely possibility that it will achieve nothing." Sing stood at the doorway and looked down the corridor.

"Maybe you should have taken up my offer to help you with those pants."

"Why?"

"Oh... no reason. I'll be downstairs if you need me."

"What? Where are you going now?" he asked as she hurried away. She disappeared without answering. "Man, she's a strange cat," he said to himself. He went out to the hallway, and found it quiet, but for one familiar face. Robert saw why Sing had fled. He looked down at his powder-flecked pants, feeling a twist of irony.

"President Summers, I had no idea you were coming, I would have..."

"Easy, Robert, surprise is the whole idea. It's a personal touch. I came to talk to you about what we're going to do." He glanced at Robert's pants. "What the hell did you do to yourself?"

"I'm masking our failure to make progress by humiliating myself."

"You're doing a damn good job of it. I haven't thought of anything else since I saw your pants. Ok, that didn't sound right. Anyway, I'm sorry to bring this up but I need to know something." President Summers paused before asking his next question. "Project Blue Star, could it be made operational again?"

The request surprised Robert. "Yeah, I—."

"Don't worry about answering me right now. I know what your worries are, just... think about it." President Summers quickly changed the subject, "I need you to oversee. You are going to head up the new rocket system that will take our people to the moon-- Project Atlantis. Any questions?"

"Yeah, I—"

"Great. That settles that. Well, Mister Director, looks like you have some directing to do. You have access to anything and anyone you need. One last thing: Get a new suit, you're going to need it. You will be at the White House in two weeks and bring that pretty Asian girl I saw running down the hallway."

"You mean Dr. Howell."

"Yes; make sure she's there. A car will pick you both up two weeks from Saturday at 5 a.m. And be ready to go. Between now and then work out a design. Have it to me in writing when you show up. We need to start construction yesterday."

"Yes, Mr. President." Summers got up to leave. Before exiting, he turned and said, "Oh and Robert."

"Yes, Mr. President."

"Get your pants cleaned."

"Yes sir."

Robert felt drained as he went to the men's room. President Andrew Summers had been the head of Allied Bomber Command, when Robert first worked for him. In those days Robert called him 'General Summers.' The General had given him authority over the German V2 recovery team. Now Project Atlantis—the moon mission-- topped the agenda. Andrew Summers wouldn't accept failure.

Robert settled back in his plush chair, feeling the weariness of the last week. In moments he was asleep. He would've stayed that way had Sing not given him a swift kick.

"What... Oh, it's you, what time is it?"

"Time for you to wake up. Working hard on that rocket, I see."

"Well, kind of, yes. I was waiting for a phone call, then I don't know what happened. You know that's the second time you've disturbed my sleep today. I'm not sure you want to know what will happen the third time."

"You know, Robert, Doctor Sum might have been onto something."

"How could 'Surrender the Earth Women' have anything to do with waking me up?"

"Hard to say. He is, after all, a bigger nerd than you, but I think he may have a piece to this puzzle. As for waking you, if you'd been more alert last night, I might not have to."

"Did you need something or are you here just to torment me?" Guttenberg asked.

"A little of both. Mostly just wanted you to know the signal has a directional orientation to it."

"Really? Pointed where?"

"Not sure yet, but the target isn't Earth. It's a narrow band signal that will travel far out into deep space before being overcome by Galactic background. I wanted to recommend a directional orientation and signal tracking package for the first satellite we send toward the moon--maybe some pictures."

"Anything else on that shopping list?"

"Not yet, I'll let you know."

"Hey, before you leave today, come see me. You and I are going to the White House in a couple of weeks."

"Oh... you're a hopeless romantic, a date to go to the White House! You see a girl naked once you just can't give her up, can you? After work it is. I trust you have figured out what you need to do tonight, or do I need Doctor Sum, who is an even bigger nerd than you to print out a set of instructions."

Robert tried to get a word out but it was too late. She was gone. "I—damn, she's quick," he complained aloud. "I never said anything about tonight. She's starting to turn into the spider queen; before I know it she will be using my dead corpse as an incubator for her eggs. My carcass will be feeding her young for weeks. And yet, I can't seem to say no."

Within a few short hours Dr. Howell had returned. She crossed over to him, lifted herself up and perched on his desk.

"Before you ask, second Saturday from today, be ready to leave my house at 5 a.m. The

President is sending a driver to pick us up. If you don't have any formal wear we'll need to get you some."

"So this is a date."

"Call it whatever you want. Seeing you in a formal dress will be the highlight of my day."

"Speaking of clothes, before we go to your house I need to stop at my apartment and pick up a few things."

"I don't remember inviting you."

"You didn't need to because I know that you know, that I know, you enjoy being with me. So, you ready?"

"Ok, you got me there; if I struggle it'll only serve to trap me completely in your web." Robert held up his hands as if to form a web.

"Oh good Lord, Robert, knock it off. If you don't want to see any of this just let me know," Sing reached down and pulled her skirt up a little farther, showing off more of her bare legs. Robert didn't say anything. He touched her leg. With a quick slap on the hand, Sing grabbed his chin with her thumb and four fingers and directed his eyes up to hers.

"Not here, Robert, at least not right now, so... shall we go?" With an ear-to-ear smile Robert headed for his car. He opened the passenger door for Sing. "My lady, your carriage awaits."

"Good boy, Robert."

Chapter Nine

Villains and Killer Clowns

Sing lived in a single bedroom apartment only minutes away from NARC labs. Most days she walked to and from work. Standing at the door of her apartment with keys in hand, she stopped for a few seconds. "Robert, I just want to warn you before we go in, it's not very fancy."

"Don't worry about it. We all start somewhere," Robert said.

"Ok, here we go." She turned the key and opened the door, only to let out a scream. Robert instinctively grabbed Sing, forcing her behind him. He peered into the apartment.

"Stay behind me," he said. His voice was one that Sing had never heard. She entered, only inches behind him.

Someone had turned her apartment upside down. Everything that wasn't nailed down lay scattered all over the floor. Tears rolled down Sing's cheeks. "Who would do this? Everything is ruined, everything…"

"If you are going to try and salvage anything I suggest you do it quickly. I'd be willing to bet we're being watched."

She ran through the apartment, finding what clothes and toiletries she could use.

"Robert, we really should call someone."

"No! Don't use the phone. The line is probably tapped. I've seen this before. Ready? We'll stop at a pay phone on the way to my house; let's get moving." He peeked outside. "It looks ok, but we won't know for sure till we are on the road." He turned to her. "Ok, when I open the door we're going to run for my car, understand?"

Sing nodded her assent.

"Alright," Robert breathed. "Let's go."

They ran for the car, Robert got in first, starting the engine as Sing jumped in. As they sped away she started crying again.

"I'm so, so, sorry, Sing. I'm not sure what happened back there. You're going to be safe, ok?" Robert rubbed her shoulder as he drove. "Hang on for just a little longer. Once we're sure no one's following, I'll stop and call the FBI." After ten minutes of random streets and driving in circles, Robert felt safe enough to stop at a pay phone. Before getting out, he said: "Sing, I need you to watch. Roll your window down, and yell if you see anything suspicious. Ready?"

"Yeah..." she gasped.

It was the best he could hope for. Robert hurried to the phone. Sing could hear his end of the call: "Hello, operator, I need to make an emergency call to the FBI. Ok.... Hello, this is Director Robert J Guttenberg of the NARC. I'm declaring a code zero, that's right, code zero. I believe I'm in danger. Roger that, you're carrying out code zero, thank you." He hung up and hurried to the car.

Sing waited until they were headed for Robert's house to talk. "What... what's code zero?"

"It'll lock down everything and everyone associated with the project. Someone will show up at my house within an hour—an agent. We should be fine from here on out."

Sing stared blankly out the passenger window. "Robert, I don't want to go back to my apartment."

"Don't worry. You can stay with me as long as you like, you know that."

"Thank you," she said, her voice still shaky.

"Try to relax. We'll be at my place in a few minutes."

By the time Robert pulled into his driveway the sun had set. Sing dozed from exhaustion, her head falling against the passenger-side window. The house looked dark. Leaving Sing in the car, Robert searched his pocket for his house key. As his fingers fumbled blindly, he suddenly realized the door was already unlocked. Pushing the door open, Robert glanced inside, but saw nothing askew. He sometimes forgot to lock up in the morning.

He went back to the car, and decided to carry Sing in. He hoisted her into his arms so carefully that she didn't stir. Only as they approached the door did her eyes begin to flutter and open.

"You are a true gentleman, Robert," She murmured as they crossed the threshold.

"You're only saying that because I haven't dropped you," he replied, heading for the couch.

He'd just set her down when Sing let out a bloodcurdling scream. Robert followed her stare. Standing in the shadows stood a man in dark clothing. A long cloth wrapped around his head, masking all but his wildly glinting eyes. The stranger's startled glance darted from Sing to the open door. Suddenly he ran, racing out into the night.

Robert flicked a light switch, only to realize there was no power. "Hold on, I have my lighter," he said, flipping open his Zippo. He lit a candle on the mantle above the fireplace. Once Robert had lit a second candle on top of the liquor cabinet, he felt a little better, "Ok," he said, keeping his voice level to calm Sing. "He's gone. I'll check the fuse box."

Sing watched as Robert disappeared into the kitchen. Within seconds, all the lights came back on. When he returned, he asked her: "Do you want a drink?"

Sing stood there for a few seconds, still adjusting to consciousness. "What...the...hell..." She stood up, looked around, then sank back onto the couch. "Wow, I mean... well...wow!" She huddled into a ball, as if she were cold. Robert thought she might be in shock.

"Sing, here, this will help," Robert said, handing her a glass of scotch. He sat down next to her. "We're ok. If they wanted to hurt us they could have done that already." He glanced around the living room and kitchen. "Something's odd about all this," he said, after looking around the house. "They didn't take anything; they may just be looking for information. Sing, you notice anything peculiar about what just happened?"

"What? Other than the fact that he didn't shut the door on his way out," Sing said in a dry tone. The shock was wearing off.

"Looks like that scotch is doing its job," said Robert. "Have another, and maybe you'll become fully functional."

"It's definitely having a numbing effect," she replied, "if that's what you mean by 'functional'. I plan on functioning like this all night."

"Ok, I'll give you some time to relax. That intruder was--how should I say-- odd. That mask looked as if it was made from a cloth flour sack. I always assumed that any foreign government that could effectively spy on us would cover their tracks well enough that they would leave no trace. Yet this guy, and whoever was at your place haven't been exactly undercover. He looked like he'd pulled his costume off a clothesline."

Sing settled in against Robert. "Maybe he was just looking for an Asian beauty ready for some action. He has a taste for the exotic."

Robert rolled his eyes. Gently shoving Sing into the couch cushions, he got up, and looked around the room. Sing murmured something, closed her eyes, and fell asleep. Robert closed the front door, then began a full inspection of his house. When he got back to the living room Sing was sitting up. She glanced at the front entrance. Robert flipped the lock, and put on the chain.

"Nothing like shutting the barn door after the horse is gone," Sing commented.

"Hey, I thought you were going to sleep."

"I am, sort of... What are you doing?"

"What am I doing?" He paused and thought about what exactly he was trying to do. "Just making sure there are no more surprises. When I was a kid I hated playing with a jack-in-the-box, and now I hate it when uninvited strangers pop up in my home."

Sing laughed. "I've seen a jack-in-the-box. Nothing more horrific than scary clowns jumping out at you."

"If you don't mind I need to finish checking the rest of the house."

"Ok, but don't say I didn't warn you about those killer clowns."

"Scary clowns I can handle. Scary guys in the dark might be different." Robert looked around. Spotting a large wooden spoon on the kitchen table he grabbed it, and clutched it like a weapon.

"What are you going to do with that? Paddle the man?" Sing asked.

"It's all I've got."

"Maybe you shouldn't have shut the front door."

"Really, you think so?"

"I am just kidding; go check the house."

"You check the house, if you're so brave."

"I would but I think I'm too drunk, Robert. If you hadn't plied me with scotch maybe I could…" She trailed off, seeming to sink back into slumber.

Robert looked at the beautiful woman. "I could use you as a decoy while I escape," he said.

"Never work," she mumbled without opening her eyes. "They find out I was more trouble than it's worth. Why are you still standing there?"

"I'm going, I'm going," he said.

He explored each room carefully, turning on every light as he entered, then switching them off as he left. Finally, after he was satisfied, he returned to Sing. "No sign of anyone," he said. "I had cash on my dresser. I think they may have moved it, but they didn't steal any. I think he was looking for information. That's probably what happened at your place too, but we didn't interrupt them there. They were already done—or he was done." He sighed. "Now, we just need to find out what they're looking for. That might tell us who's looking."

"Isn't this a job for the FBI?" sing asked. "And aren't we waiting for them?"

"Sure, but it starts right here, with us."

"Right," said Sing. "And so far we've learned… nothing."

"You have a point. Maybe we should wait for the FBI," Robert agreed.

A knock came at the door. "That might be them," said Sing. Her point was confirmed when two men burst into the room, guns drawn.

The first agent boomed: "FBI, hands where we can see them. No sudden moves and everyone will be ok. Understood?"

Robert and Sing both nodded. "My ID is in my pocket," Robert said.

"Get it out slowly."

The agents relaxed after verifying Robert and Sing's identities.

"Everything looks to be in order," said the lead agent, handing Robert his driver's license. "Sorry for the surprise. Operation Zero requires us to suspect anyone. I'm sure you understand. I'm Agent 15, and this," he nodded at his partner, "is 16 . Obviously we got your call, Dr. Guttenberg. We have two agents checking out the lady's apartment right now. I hope you don't mind if we have a look around."

"Sure, but you just missed him," Robert said.

"Missed who, sir?"

"The intruder who was here when we arrived. We've only been here a few minutes."

"You never reported someone in your house," said Agent 15.

"That's what I mean. We just arrived and you just missed him."

"Ok, ok. Please, sir, give it to me from the top."

Robert paused and collected his thoughts. "Sing and I found her apartment ransacked. We went to a phone and called your offices, then we drove here. I found my door unlocked."

"Unlocked, you say?" agent 15 said, taking notes. "Any marks on the lock or door frame?"

"I hadn't checked yet," said Robert. "Usually I lock it before leaving for work but not always. This is usually a safe area."

The agents nodded, both of them scribbling.

"Sing was asleep, so after I opened the front door, I went back to the car, picked her up, and carried her in here."

"You carried her in?" asked 16, smirking.

Sing made a gesture like a clawing cat, and hissed at the agent.

Agent 15 tried to keep the interview businesslike. "Go on, Dr. Guttenberg."

"I was concerned about Sing. Seeing her home broken into seemed to put her into shock, so I brought her here in hopes that being away from all that would calm her down. Anyway, I brought her in, and I'd just set her on the couch when she started screaming. I looked around to see someone standing right there—" he pointed "—looking back at us. He wore some kind of mask or disguise that looked like strips of sack material, or maybe torn bed sheets. The only thing we could see was his eyes. They were wild... probably scared. He stood there for a few seconds, then ran out the front door."

The agents took more notes, and Agent 15 asked: "Anything missing, damaged, out of the ordinary?"

"Not that I could tell. Whoever it was had the opportunity to steal a fair amount of cash on my dresser. They may have moved it to one side, but they didn't take it. It was all there."

"Ok," said Agent 15, putting his pad in his pocket. "We'll have that look around now."

"Go right ahead."

Agent 15 went to the door, and spoke to someone outside. "Interior is secure, proceed with exterior. Use extreme caution."

A voice reported back from the darkness, "Roger that, 15, locking down exterior." The headlights of two cars blazed, lighting up the exterior. Robert thought he could see about a half a dozen flashlights.

"16, check the house out. I'll keep a watch over these two."

"Roger that, sir," 16 replied.

Sing looked at 15. "So tell me agent...why numbers and not names? Or did the government remove those at birth?"

The agent took in a deep breath. "If you don't mind, Doctor, please refrain from asking any more questions. It's simply a matter of security."

"I see. Our security or yours?"

"This will soon be over," he said as Agent 16 returned. "In the meantime your cooperation is appreciated."

"Nothing to report," said 16. "It's just like the doctor said, cash intact, belongings intact. That's it."

"Good work, 16. Radio Central with the update.

"Yes sir," 16 said, exiting.

Agent 15 turned back to Sing and Robert. "If you will excuse me, doctors, I will be leaving you. If you need anything, we'll be set up outside for the night."

With that he tipped his hat, turned and walked out, closing the door softly.

Robert spoke first, "Finally, someone that knows how to shut a door."

"Yeah, do you think we could train him to do other tricks?"

"Oh, just stop." Robert paused, taking a quick breath. He gently touched her shoulder and looked her in the eyes. "It looks like you have gotten over your earlier shock, but I want you tell me the truth. How are you?"

"I'm fine," she said, "though a few days of peace and quiet wouldn't hurt either of us."

"I can't agree more. I, for one, am looking forward to a quiet night. Maybe with our new friends out there, we'll have one."
Robert sank into his favorite leather chair. Within moments he was fast asleep.

"Nothing left for this girl to do but pour myself a drink and head for the bath," Sing told herself.

She headed to the bath with the bottle, leaving the glass behind.

"Why use a glass when no one's there to refill it?" Sing started undressing as she walked down the hall. After a few gulps from the bottle she was down to pantyhose. She arrived at the bathroom, the bottle loose in her fingers. Most men would have sat up to take notice, but the only man in the house was sound asleep.

Chapter Ten

Surreal Visitations

Sing slid into the bathtub, bottle of scotch still in hand. She'd found some bubble bath, and wondered if it were Robert's, or a leftover from a previous tenant.

"This is more like it," she said as she immersed herself. The combination of alcohol and warm bubbly water soothed her. She lay in a cloud of bubbles, her arm hanging over the side, still holding the scotch bottle. Sing closed her eyes and relaxed. The alcohol would help her forget, if only for a little while. The longer she stayed, the more she drank. She no longer felt numb to the world, and she realized she was passing into a different place, a location beyond feeling or sensation. She couldn't even feel the water anymore. When she realized she may have drunk too much she tried to pull the bottle up to her face to see how much was left. After a second try the bottle made it up to the bath only to slip from her hand and land in the bath water.

She let out a yell, "Oh Shooooooo...t," then laughed profusely until she heard a knock at the front door.

"Oh, uh, hey Robert," she yelled, "Robert!"

From the other room came nothing but silence . Sing tried to get out of the bath but couldn't find the strength or stability to rise.

"Damn, that sleeping bear," she grumbled. She gave a feeble yell: "Hey, come on, come in!"

She could hear the sound of the front door opening.

"Uh, hello. Sorry to come so late. Hello," said a voice that sounded like that of an older man.

"Uh, in here," Sing called.

"Oh, ok I coming. So sorry to show up so late." The stranger headed for the sound of Sing's voice. As he approached the bathroom door he kept talking. "It regretful, but they call my home.

The FBI say you need a tailor immediately. Sincerest apologies. I'm so late, if I heard earlier, I would have arrived... OH MY!" He stood in the bathroom door staring at her. "If this is a bad time I come back later. By the looks of things maybe I should."

"Wait, please, I'm Doctor Sing. That bear sleeping in the chair is Doctor Guttenberg, Director of the NARC." She reached out to shake the man's hand, but only splashed soapy water on him.

"Ok, I'll come back later. Goodbye."

"Hey wait—maybe you should wake him up," she flung her hand in a random direction. "Tell me, if you will, why you are here?"

"I received a call."

"We didn't call."

"What, you no call? FBI say it was urgent. Come, they say, come now."

"Ok, Ok, wake that guy out there in the living room. Tell him to help me out of this bathtub."

Sing slumped back down. "Fine day for visitors," she said while checking the contents of the scotch bottle. How had it gotten so empty?

The man went out to the living room, and gently nudged Robert. "Wake up, sir, wake…. girl in bath needs you."

Robert stirred, wondering what dream this was. He wasn't used to strangers waking him in his own home. Though his vision was blurred by sleep, he saw a short Asian man in his forties, wearing a dark colored three-piece suit, and sporting a matching hat. Robert rubbed his eyes. "What, girl? What… Who are you, anyway?"

The man stepped back, and removed his hat. "Sir, I apologize for the late hour. My name is Benjamin Lee. I received phone call to come here at once and take your measurements."

"My what?" Robert said, suddenly awake.

"Measurements, I am a tailor that contracts for FBI. They told me had to be done tonight. I talked to the lady in the other room and she told me to wake you. She is very beautiful lady, sir, but she cannot climb out of bathtub and…" he looked down at the floor for a second. "She said you... help her from the bath. You know, can't get out."

"She's in the bath?"

"Yes sir."

Robert wrestled himself out of his chair.

"Why can't she get out of the tub?"

"Maybe she drink too much. I don't know, I thought I see bottle of scotch floating..."

Heading for the bathroom Robert thought to ask, "She didn't take a bath with her clothes on, did she?"

Benjamin looked a little embarrassed, "I—I no think so..."

Benjamin followed Robert into the bathroom.

"Hey, gentlemen, you're just in time. I drained the water, thinking one of you might take a moment to help me out."

Sing lay in the bottom of the bathtub, clothed only in a thin layer of bubbles.

"Benjamin, hand me one of those towels behind you," said Robert.

"Oh, yes of course. Here you go. If you not need me I wait in other room. Give you and your wife privacy."

"She's not my wife," Robert said. "She's... oh, never mind. Good idea, just wait for me out there. I'll be with you in a few minutes."

Sing spoke up drunkenly, "If I was his wife I'd be one fine catch, wouldn't I."

Kneeling down next to the tub, Robert started wiping the soap off of Sing's body. The empty bottle of scotch in the bottom of the bathtub painted a complete picture.

"You definitely need someone to take care of you, that's for sure. Lift your arms, ok?"

Throwing the towel over his shoulder, Robert reached down, rolled Sing up and out of the tub and onto his shoulder, carrying her to his bedroom where he laid her on his bed. Looking around he found a white undershirt.

"Here we go, Can't have you running around naked, can I?" Robert said, holding her long enough to get a shirt on. "I don't have anything else for the rest of you. I am just going to use this towel. As long as you don't get too busy it should hold around your midsection."

"Robert."

"Yes, Sing."

"I feel sick."

"Ok.... I didn't want to hear that. Hey Benjamin, if you are going to take measurements, better get started."

The voice from the living room said, "Oh, yes sir, it won't take but a few minute for both of you." Benjamin walked in with a small bag and a note pad. He worked on Sing first.

"The FBI ordered this?" Robert asked.

"Indeed, I have crew ready, soon as I call in."

"We aren't leaving for Washington for a couple of weeks. So why measure us tonight?"

"Sorry, I no help there. Please, stand up. I need honorable measurements on woman, and on you."

"Sure."

As he finished his work, he flipped through his notebook and penciled in a few numbers. "Mister, I finished here. I leave you and your – friend. Goodnight to you, sir." Benjamin wasted no time in leaving.

After his departure, Sing spoke up. "Who was that, Robert?"

"Said he was a tailor, but I don't really know. Had an interesting accent--maybe Mandarin. Hard to tell really..." He glanced down to see that Sing was sound asleep again. "Well, I don't think she'll cause anymore trouble tonight. I'll put her in my bed." He looked her up and down. "Second time I've seen her naked, but I'll do the gentlemanly thing and sleep on the couch." He halted. "Waita minute. My house, my bed. No reason to sleep alone tonight..." Despite the distraction of a beautiful naked woman, he fell asleep the moment his head hit the pillow.

Sometime later he woke to yet another strange voice: "Sir... mister, uh – hi. Sorry to wake you, sir."

Robert opened his eyes. The room was dark and the house was quiet, but someone stood at the foot of his bed, holding a lit cigarette. On the other side of the bed he could see Sing sleeping soundly. He laid his head back down, uncertain why he was awake.

The voice spoke again: "Sir, we need to leave in one hour. You and your wife need to be ready to leave at that time."

Lifting his head off the pillow Robert came fully awake. "I told you earlier, she's not my wife."

The stranger drew on his cigarette, and exhaled smoke. "Hmm... no, don't think so. Matter of fact I don't think I've ever met you before this minute."

The only light in the room was the glowing ash on the stranger's cigarette. Robert propped himself up on his elbows and tried to make sense of this shadow man. "I didn't tell you?"

"Nope," the stranger replied.

"Oh, well ok, so... why are you in my room?"

"I'm your driver."

"My what?"

"Your driver."

"I don't have a driver."

"You do now. We leave in an hour. I suggest you and your not-wife get ready."

"The time, do you have the time?"

"Yeah, 2 AM," the man said finishing his cigarette. "I'll be outside waiting for you and this woman who's not your wife."

"2 AM? Where are we going?"

"Look, pal, I don't know your ultimate destination. I was told to take you to the airport, so I'm here to do it. Anymore questions, ask the pilot—maybe he'll know. No more questions. Just be outside in an hour."

Robert watched the shadowy stranger leave. "What is it with my house? They open my front door uninvited, but can't remember how to close it." He turned on a dim lamp and gazed at Sing. "She's peaceful when she sleeps; it's when she's awake that troubles me."

She slept on her side facing Robert. He hated waking anyone after a heavy night of drinking, and he hesitated now. Taking her hand, Robert gently rubbed it. "Hey, hey, Sing, wake up darling, wake up. Come on, wake up."

Sing stirred only slightly. Trying again, gently patting her left cheek, he drew mixed results. A hand waved from the sheets, trying to hit something, then withdrew. He walked through the house, turning on every light, as he shouted: "Alright, get out of that bed, Sing Ann Howell! We have thirty minutes. It would help if you got up and dressed yourself."

Sing opened her eyes. "Uh,what the...?"

"The road of life is paved with strange conditions," Robert complained to himself. Finally he rolled her up into the bed's blanket, threw her over his shoulder and headed for the door.

Chapter Eleven

Reaching for the Stars (Again)

Carrying Sing from the car to the airplane hadn't been easy. Though she wasn't heavy, her legs and arms flopped in all directions. Robert had just gotten her strapped into her seat when a gentleman carrying a suit for him and a fine dress for Sing boarded the plane.

"Have these on when you land," the man said tersely, then left.

Robert called after him: "What about her? She is in no condition to dress herself right now."

Reaching the exit door the man turned, smiled, and said, "I think you can handle that." He hurried out the exit.

As Robert explored the plane, he found two armed Air Force officers in the cockpit. "Actual human pilots," he said.

Ignoring Robert's comment, the first officer addressed him. "Have a seat, Director Guttenberg; we'll be taking off as soon as preflight is finished."

"Anyone want to tell me where we're going?"

"Sure, as soon as we know."

"What? You don't know where we're going?"

"Nope, you see this sealed envelope?"

"Yeah."

"If you would be so kind as to close that hatch next to you, we're going to open this, and read our instructions. We hope it'll tell us where we're going."

"You hope?"

"They don't always tell us on missions like this. Usually there's a series of coded checkpoints each leading to the next. So, if you don't mind, Doctor, the hatch..."

"Hmm, yes, of course."

Robert reached out grabbed the handle attached to a set of steps. When he pulled the stairs retracted and the door came up. He moved the red lever to the locked position. The pilot registered a green light on his instrument panel.

"Good job, doctor, now I need you to take a seat."

"I thought you were going to tell me where we're going."

"I sure will, just after we land."

The copilot opened the letter and turned to Robert.

"Director Guttenberg, be patient. You will know a lot more than we do in the next few hours." He glanced at his instructions. "Probably about three hours, based on what I see here. The first stop will be Dr. Howell's. Have her in that dress and ready to go when we land. For now, just sit down, relax, and maybe take a nap--it looks like you could use it. I will let you know when it's safe to play dress up."

The pilots laughed and turned back to their preflight routine.

Once Robert was seated, the buzz of the aircraft's twin engines settled into background noise, and he fell asleep. They were the only passengers en route to an unknown destination on a twin-engine DC-3. The plane displayed no distinguishing marks.

Sometime later a change in the sound of the engines woke Robert. Judging by the sound, he believed the plane had reached its cruising altitude. Lifting his head he could see Sing looking out the window. She was awake now, and Robert felt relief. He hadn't looked forward to changing her clothes for her.

"How are you feeling?" he asked her.

"Just a little under the weather."

Sing got up, and started changing her clothes. Once she asked Robert to steady her as they hit minor turbulence. When she was done, he gazed at her. "You look beautiful in that dress," he said.

"Thank you," she said. "I'm not sure why I need to wear it, but I do like the way it fits. Whoever guessed my size did a great job."

Robert looked uncomfortable.

"Ok, what are you not telling me? Come on, 'fess up. I wake up in a plane already in flight, with you hovering over me like a mama hen, asking me to put on a dress I've never seen before. What gives?"

"I don't know what's happening, or where we're going," said Robert, "but last night a man showed up to take our measurements. He alerted me to the fact that you needed help out of the bath. Why he knew this I don't know. You must have said something to him. After seeing an empty bottle of scotch floating next to you, I could see why."

Sing laughed. "I do remember grabbing the scotch, but it all goes blank from there. How did I get here, wearing only a t-shirt and a blanket? I didn't plan on wearing anything anytime soon." Sing winked at Robert. "So what gives?"

"I don't know," he admitted. "I just hope I haven't led you into something dangerous."

She took his hand. "Robert, I couldn't feel safer around any other man."

The roar from the engines deepened as they descended. Morning sun shone over the horizon, bathing the rear of the airplane in bright orange light.

"I'm not sure where you're headed," Robert told Sing," but they're dropping you off here. When we meet up at the lab again we need to talk about you and me. If you want to stay with me, nothing would make me happier than waking up to you every day."

Sing leaned over from her seat, and gave Robert a hug, and a long, lingering kiss.

"Robert."

"Yes, Sing."

"I will think about it," she said, still hugging him.

The plane made its approach to what looked like a military air field. They taxied a short distance and came to a complete stop at the end of the runway. A car was waiting.

"They're not wasting any time, are they?" said Sing.

Sing stood up. Two men boarded. Sing's eyes grew large.

"What is it, Sing?" Robert asked.

"I'm not sure, but this is highly irregular."

"What do you mean?"

"These men are Japanese—former military, or government security." Sing glanced out the portal, and saw the well-dressed man waiting in the car's backseat. She climbed past Robert to the center aisle. "This should be good," she said softly.

The lead man addressed her: "Dr. Howell." He bowed as a subordinate would. "The Japanese Ambassador to the United States requests you accompany him."

Sing bowed back slightly. By Japanese custom they were showing respect for her.

"This can't be all bad," Sing said to Robert. "They told me I'm boss. It's about time."

"Don't let it go to your head; I'm sure they have some surprises in store for you."

"No doubt. Ok, wish me luck."

"Good luck, Sing," Robert said, watching her exit the aircraft.

As Robert stood to stretch his legs a voice came over the speaker: "You ok back there, Doctor?"

"Just stretching my legs," he called in the direction of the cockpit.

"Good. Take a seat. We'll take off momentarily."

"Just out of curiosity, how much longer?" Robert asked.

"You'll know when we get there, Director. I wish I could tell you more, but we don't know much ourselves. Just sit tight. It won't be too long. This plane only holds so much fuel."

The moment Robert sat down he felt the aircraft moving again. As the engines pulsed with power, he hoped this would be a short hop. *Nothing like an unknown destination and a short night to disturb a man's sleep,* he mused before drifting away.

He woke to an urgent voice from the speaker. "Director Guttenberg, wake up and strap in. We are headed for a hard landing! We are on approach and out of fuel."

Robert buckled up, and glanced outside. Visibility was poor, and there was sporadic lightning. They passed over shapes and shadows of what might be buildings. A sharp jolt rocked the plane. There was no crash. They'd settled onto a runway.

The pilot reported: "We're on the ground in one piece. Sorry to scare you. Between wind and visibility we couldn't land on our first approaches. While circling we ran low on fuel. We almost pumped the tanks dry on our final approach."

Robert got up, and saw the pilot come out to the forward hatch. As Robert joined him, the sound of rain echoing off the aluminum skin of the plane was deafening. Robert looked out at a grey landscape. "What have I gotten myself into?"

He stepped out, started down the steps; by the time he reached the tarmac he was soaked. "Today's just not my day, is it?" A shadow appeared in the grayness. "Oh, hello, who's this?"

It was a young lady sporting a bright pink umbrella and rain boots. "Director Guttenberg? My name is Mary Ann, personal assistant to President Summers. If you would follow me."

Robert trudged through the rain feeling as gray as the weather. His new suit clung to his skin. Mary Ann guided him without conversation. They entered a building equipped with giant sliding doors. Having spent many years working in buildings just like it, Robert knew the design. It gave him a sense of déjà vu. Every airfield used hangers like this one.

Though Robert knew this must be the airport's main hanger, it stunk of disuse. Stale air permeated his nostrils. Layers of dust covered every flat surface. All-in-all it seemed like a place that had passed its prime.

Robert turned to Mary Ann, "This place hasn't been used in years," he said. "Why are we here?"

"Please be patient, Director," Mary Ann said, as she set up a portable table. "President Summers will be here shortly."

The rain had soaked through his clothes chilling him. As he noted the many wooden shipping crates, he shoved his hands into his pockets. Then came the surprise in the form of a warm rich aroma.

"Director Guttenberg, coffee is ready," Mary said.

"Just what I need."

Robert stopped suddenly at a blue and white sign with a giant blue star centered inside a black border. It read, *Success comes from trying things others dismiss out of hand.*

He was hit by a memory that left him weak. Once he'd called this place home. It wasn't a residence, nor was it simply a workplace. It had been a dream. He'd known a place just like this many years earlier, in Jackson, Ohio. That had been a nondescript air field buried deep in farm country. When the memory stirred up waves of emotion, Robert tried a process of thought neutralization, hoping it would smooth out competing feelings. It didn't.

"Project Blue Star," he muttered. "I had... no idea..."

"That's right, Robert," a voice answered. Robert glanced around to find President Summers coming in out of the rain. "Simple question, Robert. We've known each other long enough to know what the answer is. If I asked you to volunteer to return to one of your old stomping grounds would you go?"

Robert said nothing.

"Just as I thought," said Summers. "Here, take a seat. We need to talk. How long have we known each other, Robert?"

"Thirteen years, maybe fourteen."

"And in that time you've had a great career. But Blue Star wasn't part of it. Blue Star didn't work out. But that wasn't your fault. Competing interests tried to rob you of what you accomplished. They managed to halt the whole project."

Robert shook his head. This was where he'd worked to fully develop German rocket designs. They'd come close. If they'd had another eighteen months they could've put sent the first rocket to the edge of outer space.

"Robert, you are the Albert Einstein of rocketry," President Summers said.

Andrew Summers' love of aviation had led him to the command of allied bombing, but his real dream was manned flight to the moon. When he'd realized that Robert Guttenberg could look over a V2 rocket, then draw exact blueprints from memory several months later, Summers knew he needed this man. But it hadn't gone well for Robert.

"The past is the past. Why can't anyone understand that?" Robert asked.

"Sometimes, Robert, the past is a guidepost to the future," President Summers said. "You wrote those words on that sign back '48, and it made me believe in you. I know you haven't forgotten; that's why we're here today."

"Yes, Mr. President," Robert said, staring at the floor.

"Your days of calling me 'Mr. President' are over. We both lost close friends in the war. But we wanted the aftermath to have meaning. The words on that sign are more true today than they ever were."

"Mr. President..."

"Robert, call me Andrew. We're equals, and we both believe humanity can reach the stars. Project Blue Star was the natural evolution of that dream."

"I know, I know," Robert said. "It moved too fast, we made great strides, but an atomic engine..." Robert trailed off. The Blue Star program had been their attempt to find an atomic solution to the challenges of space travel, but demands for glory had usurped the urge to do good. When those forces found themselves having to explain the deaths of scientists and other project workers, they put the blame squarely on Robert, and destroyed the project.

Now he looked at the hangar as if it were a funeral pyre. Yet he sensed a phoenix could rise from those dying embers. Somehow the terrible memories might be eclipsed by hope.

"Andrew," Robert asked, "why are we here?"

"You said it yourself. We may not be alone and if Atlantis is going to take years, we need to find a second option. We have one asset we could mobilize quickly: we need to know what's out there. Something's happening that affects us. We must learn what it is."

Robert crossed his arms. "I've learned some things the hard way. If you want me to lead this project, I must have complete authority—in writing. There's no other option."

"Granted," said Summers. "Anything else?"

"Yes, I need Sing. If anyone is going to unlock that signal and find out what it's for, it will be Sing."

"Alright, staff is completely your call. Continue."

"Then there's money. We'll need a lot. Every piece of hardware, electronics, you name it—needs to be retooled or replaced. We're talking about a forty-year advance in a few short months. I don't know how we'll do it, but I think we can—with funds."

The President sipped coffee, and gave this some thought. "Ok," he said. "You'll have all the support you need. I'm leaving Tom with you."

A man dressed in khaki pants and a dark leather bomber jacket step out of the shadows. He saluted them both, and nodded to Summers.

"Tom Dangerfield," he said, facing Robert.

They shook hand.

"Use him," said Summers. "Tom reports directly to me, if you understand what I'm saying. He's one of the best pilots I know. If there's a flaw in anything you build, Tom can sniff it out before it leaves the ground."

"You're willing to give me unrestricted authority?" Robert asked.

"And resources. I know I don't need to tell you, time is not our friend. It's up to you and NARC. You have an office in D.C. whenever you need it, and as you get the governmental gears moving, I'll be backing you every step of the way. But it will be an incredible challenge—the biggest you've ever faced. With such a tight schedule, you need to get to know one another right now." Summers slapped his leg and stood up. "You can start over these pastries from the White House kitchen. They might be the only fringe benefit you'll see." Summers smiled, nodded, and walked out without saying good-bye.

Chapter Twelve

Redux of Project Blue Star, Fall, 1959

Doctor Guttenberg sat on a hard wooden bench waiting to catch the 9:40 train out of Washington D.C. His watch read, 9:15 a.m. The choice to sit outside was clear; with cooler weather most of the passengers had sought the comfort of a warm building, but not the Doctor. The cool fall winds had provided him a source of solitude. Wrapped up in his coat, he kept warm with a cup of hot coffee from the station's cantina. The solitude provided Robert time to focus on something he enjoyed every fall: watching the leaves cover the ground with bright colors. He tugged on his hat, pulling it down tight so the wind wouldn't take it. Robert didn't mind the wind.

A woman approached and took a seat in the open space next to him. At first he resented her presence as an intrusion on his thoughts, but then he saw something tantalizing: a patch of skin. The woman's ankles were bare, as were her legs up to her knees. She wore her coat carelessly, and it wasn't clear if she had anything on beneath it. Robert watched without moving his head, trying to sneak a peek at her thighs, then he realized she was staring directly at him. He glanced about nervously as she uncrossed and re-crossed her legs. Robert felt he must say something polite, but he didn't know what. His eyes met hers.

The strength of her gaze startled him. She wore a fine Boucle Camel-colored coat with wide fur trim and a silk lining. The coat was buttoned with three large buttons. Below the last button was the gap that led to her thighs. She needed only to tug on the coat to close it completely, but she hadn't. On her feet was a chic pair of brown leather shoes, and she held a matching purse. But her expression exuded authority. Her whole demeanor gave her a commanding presence.

Just as Robert opened his mouth to speak, the radio suddenly blared over the station's loudspeakers. "This is WGN 1080. You were listening to, *It's only a Paper Moon* by Ella Fitzgerald and the Delta Rhythm Boys. Up next, Bob Crosby and the Bob Cats. They'll perform *Happy Times*. The time is now 09:25."

"Anna Urisa," the woman said softly, holding her hand out to Robert. "Interesting name, isn't it?"

"Yours or the song's?" he said.

"Ha, ha, you silly man. My name is Anna Urisa but I am talking about the song, *Happy Times*. Or is it uncustomary for me to say my name before asking you a question."

Robert sat, staring into her eyes,.

"What's the matter? Does the Felis Silvestris Catus have your tongue?" she said with a sly smile.

"What... a house cat? Where did that come... Ok, I get it," Robert stammered. "Forgive my awkwardness—I'm just ... uncertain how to approach women of your...distinction."

A gust interrupted him, and leaves swirled all around them. Anna plucked stray leaves from her coat. As she looked at Robert, he began to feel two things, one surprising, one not: desire and terror. Her beauty thrilled him and scared him at the same time.

A confident man approached the station's cantina. He was watching the Doctor. He wore khakis and a dark leather bomber jacket displaying the unit patch of Helios. It pictured a proud and attractive god circling the Earth with his sun chariot, emblazoned with the words: "Guardian of oaths."

A gust of wind mussed his carefully coiffed hair. Tom pulled out a comb to repair the damage. His attention to his hair covered up the fact that he was watching Robert and the woman. This beauty was making a subtle effort to talk to the scientist. "Apparently, my compadre needs saving," he thought to himself. He turned to the pretty girl behind the counter. "Hi," he said smoothly." My name's Tom Dangerfield. You are simply the sweetest girl I've seen in a long time. Could you do a tired traveler one favor? You see that man over there sitting on that bench?" Tom pointed. "He's a distinguished scientist, and people try to steal his secrets all the time." Tom lowered his voice. "It's my job to protect him. Even now that regal lady is pumping him for information. I need your help in separating those two."

Tom pulled some bills from his pocket and slipped them into her hand. Placing his lips into her ear, he whispered something. He gave her cheek a kiss before walking away. Standing a few yards from the woman and Robert, Tom glanced at his watch, then pretended to look for the train. Looking back at his watch, he said, loudly enough to be heard: "Darn thing. Second time it's stopped. I thought the guy fixed it!" He looked at the two people on the bench. "Would either of you have the time? This darn watch, I had it fixed a week ago but it just won't work." Tom narrowed his eyes and pointed at Robert, "Wait, I know you, you are......Doctor, Doctor Gutten.... Guttenberg, that's right. I am so sorry to disturb you miss, Miss....?"

"That's ok, you're not disturbing me--Anna, Anna Urisa," she said.

"Anna, I'm Tom Dangerfield." He stepped closer to shake her hand. "Anna Urisa, that's a very distinguished name. Where are you from, Anna?"

Anna looked at her watch, ignoring the question.

"It's 0 nine thirty, Tom."

"Oh, the time, right... You're very helpful, Anna. I'm sorry to interrupt you and the good doctor." He moved away, humming and singing along with the music from the speaker. A group sang: "Baby, its cold outside..."

The whole episode confused Robert, and he was about to say something. Then the radio stopped, and a voice called from the speaker: "Dr. Robert Guttenberg, paging Dr. Robert Guttenberg, there is an urgent call waiting for you at the Information Desk."

"What?" Tom said, looking about. "Interrupt a different song would you. Why this song? It's my favorite." As Robert got up and headed inside, Tom looked at Anna. She wore a quizzical expression as she watched Robert leave. "Can you believe they interrupted that last song?" Tom exclaimed.

"I believe that was him they were paging," Anna said.

"Oh, yes of course, you mind if I sit there?" Without waiting for an answer, Tom sat.

"I think the Doctor will be—ok," said Anna. "So you know the Doctor?"

"Of course," Tom replied. "Who doesn't know the doctor? He is the greatest man of our time, or any time... Ok, I don't really know him. Why are you so interested in him?"

"I merely sat here," she said. "But why are you so interested in me, Mister Tom? You've been watching me." As she spoke she kept her eyes on the track. A train whistle sounded. A moment later the 9:40 rolled into the station.

Tom watched her board the train.

"Tom, Tom," Robert called out as he emerged from the station. "We need to board."

"I know. This way, Robert," Tom ushered the Doctor onto the train, glancing back at the car Anna had boarded. "Let me buy you a drink," he offered. "It's going to be a long ride."

Tom took Robert toward the dining car, safely away from Anna. The car's design employed stainless steel and chrome in the sleek tradition of Streamliners. It was built for people in a hurry, but Tom wanted to keep Robert there for a while. He pulled the Doctor past the service attendant and counter, all the way to the back. There they sat at the wet bar.

As the two got established, Robert started: "Tom, the strangest thing just happened."

"Hold that thought," Tom interrupted. "What's your flavor, doctor?"

"Uh, well, how about a vodka martini."

The service attendant came back behind the bar, and smiled at them. "Good morning, gentlemen, how can I serve you on this fine morning?"

"Two vodka martinis," Tom said, grinning.

"You do know it's morning, right?" the attendant asked.

"I do, and it is a fine morning. But two stiff drinks will make our long journey shorter," Tom said.

"Make that three," said a soft supple voice. Robert turned, his fingers inadvertently brushing against her leg.

"The first touch is free, Doctor. The second will cost you," Anna said, smiling. "You two don't mind if I join you. " She took the stool next to Robert's.

"No," said Robert.

"Yes!" said Tom.

"My, my, such confusion! What's a girl to do? Maybe if I buy the first round of drinks while the two of you will decide on an answer."

"That's ok, Anna, I have this round," Tom insisted.

Anna ignored him. She made eye contact with the attendant. When he came over, she pressed a ten-dollar bill into his palm, and said: "Keep the drinks flowing. I'll pick up the tab." She added a five. "And this is for you."

"Thank you, Ma'am," he said with a subtle wink.

As the drinks arrived, Anna crossed her legs, and said: "Robert, you and your friend don't mind if I take my jacket off, do you?"

"No, why would we mind?" Tom said. He wanted to stop this conversation before it started.

"Just asking," she said, peeling off her coat. Underneath she wore a black cocktail dress that accented her figure.

Anna gave Tom a devastating smile. She exuded authority, and the total dominance of sex appeal. Tom felt outclassed, and for once he lost some of his confidence.

"Robert," she asked softly, "do you mind if I ask you a question? Back at the train station, just when I thought we were about to get acquainted, you suddenly left. Is that how you treat all the ladies?" Her knee touched his thigh.

Robert gulped down his martini. He felt flattered, but also quite awkward. He took a deep breath, and looked at this beautiful creature. There would be no comfort from her. She was looking for something, and that something might be more than companionship.

As the train picked up speed, Tom tried to think of a way to run interference for Robert. He wedged himself between the two, and noticed the cook at the griddle.

That gave Tom an idea. "Robert, you hungry? What am I saying? Of course you're hungry." He glanced at the woman. "How about you, beautiful? A delicate flower like you probably doesn't eat much."

"No," she said, "but if you're buying, Tom, I'll take pancakes, juice, two eggs, toast, a double serving of bacon oh... and maybe some coffee. Is that too much or should I forget the coffee?"

Tom kept his jaw from dropping, then nodded to the attendant, who was scribbling it down. "You can drink all the coffee you want, but we need to talk."

"Yes, we do," Anna agreed. "Robert, I'm dying to know who called you back there."

"Uh, well I'm not sure. When they handed me the phone no one was there," Robert answered. "Tom, I suspect you faked that call to peel the good Doctor away from me."

The last of Tom's confidence drained away. "Um... you got me."

"Oh, don't worry, Tom. I give you points for trying."

"Who are you?" Robert asked her.

"I'm the source of your mystery, and the key to unlocking it," she said. "I want to know if I can trust you, but Tom won't let me find out."

"What?" Tom protested, leaning in between them.

"Tom, I need you to step aside," said Robert.

"Doctor, it's my job to protect you. She's not what you think."

"I know, Tom, that's why I need you to trust me," Robert said.

"I hope you know what you're doing," Tom muttered. He gave Anna a suspicious look, and went over to the window. Staring out at the passing scenery, he stifled the urge to take the Doctor by the arm, and push him away from the woman.

Anna gripped a slip of paper. Despite her commanding air, she was now entering a situation that was beyond her control.

"Doctor Robert Guttenberg," she said, her manner becoming formal, "I am Anna Urisa, captain of the Guild ship, Urisa. We had to make an emergency landing on your moon. The message you're receiving at your facility is our distress signal." She handed the slip of paper to Robert. "Guild law forbids me to contact you, but ours is a desperate situation. We believe our signal is encountering the two-light-year limit where signal strength blends with cosmic background, making it..." she paused looking at the floor "...undetectable. That paper must be given to your Doctor Sing. She will know what to do with it."

"How do you know Doctor Sing?"

"I'm taking a great risk telling you who we are. This is the key to unlock the signal and play the message, proving what I am saying."

Robert stared at her. "Anna, I don't know what to say. You know more about me than I know about you. How can I even begin to believe this story?"

"Just use the key, Robert."

The attendant set three places on the bar, and started serving them breakfast.

"Maybe we should eat," Tom said, taking a seat. "Coffee please."

Robert didn't respond, his mind was on Doctor Sing. Despite his efforts, he hadn't been in contact with her since his last meeting with President Summers. Looking at the slip of paper he felt a deep sense of longing. Sing had become something special, something more than a friend, maybe even a lover.

Anna touched his arm. "Robert, try and trust me. We know about Project Blue Star. We'll even help you, but first you must verify that I'm telling the truth."

"I...I... uh."

"Don't say anything, Robert. I will be in contact." Anna gathered her things. "If you choose not to help us we must explore other options, but I'm hoping it doesn't come to that." She smiled gently, then turned and walked away.

When the train stopped, they watched Anna step down onto the platform. Just before she entered the station she turned and waved.

"Think we'll see her again?" Robert asked his shadow.

Tom scratched his head. "Time will tell, doctor, time will tell."

Chapter Thirteen

The Cat's Meow

Robert slumped in the back seat of a taxi, exhausted from his trip. Rain pelted the windshield.

As they turned into his driveway the driver said, "Sir, I hope you have an umbrella."

As he handed bills to the driver, Robert glanced out through the downpour. His house was dark.

"Be careful out there, sir."

"Yeah, thank you. Keep the change, and be careful."

"Thank you, sir."

As the taxi cleared the driveway, Robert stood in the rain, thinking of Sing. He'd called her from Washington, trying her at home and at work, but they never connected. He'd left messages at NARC. He'd had hoped to find her looking out from one of the windows, waiting. She wasn't there. He stood, letting rain wash feelings from his mind, his hope and excitement fading. Finally he went inside. There was the letter, addressed to him in her handwriting.

Dear Doctor Guttenberg,

Thank you for everything. Our separation in Washington has shown me just how important my contributions are. So please excuse my lack of communication but I am needed at the lab. Apparently I need to show the MEN IN CHARGE I have more value than just being a man's walking theme park with all the rides and visual entertainment. See you at the lab.

Sing

Robert set the letter on the kitchen table. Already the ink was running from the moisture on his hands.

For the next hour he communicated with a bottle of scotch. He wanted to reach for the phone, but the bottle kept winning out. Could he call her this late? Would she be asleep? Angry? Uncaring? All of these thoughts crossed his mind as he chain-smoked cigarettes and drank the scotch.

He stared down at the note again. Could it have some hidden meaning? How was he to know what she meant about anything? Robert surrendered to fear, and pushed the phone away, 'Tomorrow… maybe…tomorrow," he mumbled, stumbling to his room, "I will learn something, maybe… or not…" and he was asleep.

In the morning he still wondered, but the sunrise made him feel better. On the drive to work he began to feel almost chipper, though he had no idea why. As he walked into the lobby Peggy greeted him with surprise.

"Good morning, Doctor Guttenberg."

"It is a good morning, Peggy. Thank you for reminding me," Robert said, as if he'd never been gone.

"How was—"

"Everything was fine, Peggy… just fine."

"Uh… ok. Your newspaper is here," she said, handing him the Sun-Times. "I haven't been putting it on your desk because you weren't here."

"Of course." He took the newspaper, then said: "Would you please tell Sing to meet me in my office as soon as possible?"

He walked down the corridor with its tall plate glass windows lining one side, and a row of office doors on the other. Outside the windows Autumn was bursting with color. As he reached the door to his office he heard Peggy's on the pubic address system: "Doctor Sing Ann Howell, Doctor Sing Ann Howell, please meet Director Guttenberg in his office."

Several stories below ground Sing had been living like a vampire. She couldn't remember the last time she'd seen the sun. Though she knew it was fall, she was missing the showcase of colors. The only time she was above ground was when it was dark. She was going through documents by the light of her desk when she heard Peggy's voice echoing from the nearby speaker.

"That son of a bitch," Sing said. She dropped her cigarette to the floor and stamped it out.

Three minutes later Robert heard scratching out in the corridor. It sounded like a cat clawing a screen door. Then his office door burst open.

"You… You…" Sing stood pointing a finger at him.

"What did I do?" he said.

"What? You ask what? I can't… You lousy…"

"Sing, please, have a seat."

Sing glared at him as she plopped into one of the plush chairs by the window. She tugged angrily at her lab coat, realizing her skirt was showing a little more leg than she wanted.

"Ok, Robert, what exactly do you need?" she said crossing her arms.

"Well, it's complicated."

"What's complicated? If you know what you need just tell me so I can get back to work," she snapped.

"First of all, is there something you need to tell me?"

"Ha! Tell you! I think not," she grunted.

Robert rubbed his head. "We were doing so well before we left for Washington. What happened? Where did you go?"

"What do you mean, where did I go? I…" Sing broke down in confusion. She'd spent weeks feeling alone and abandoned. Finally she mumbled, "So, what… uh, did you need?"

"Have you ever heard of Project Blue Star?"

"No. Have you ever heard of Project Pin Cushion?"

"I'm serious."

"Of course you are," Sing said "I'm serious too. Tell me about Blue Star, and I'll tell you about Pin Cushion."

"Pin Cushion? Sing, what are you talking about?"

"You leave me with men who wanted to use me like a seamstress uses a pin."

"A seamstress?" Robert said, then he got it.

"Oh my gosh," Robert gasped. "They didn't... you didn't... I'm so sorry, Sing. I had no idea."

"Relax, Robert. I'm still here and I'm ok. And for some crazy reason I believe you." Her gaze shifted from him to the still-folded newspaper on his desk. "Hey, what's that?" Suddenly Sing was out of her seat, and grabbing the paper from Robert's desk. "What is this, Robert? The first image of the far side of the moon!" She set the paper in front of him, and pointed to the grainy image. "How long was it going to take for you to tell me?"

He glanced down. "That? It just came in last night from Tass in Moscow. Their Lunik Three took the image. But we're running out of time, Sing. That's why I need to talk to you about Project Blue Star."

"Ok, go ahead, Robert," Sing said, her confusion complete. She sat back down, trying to make sense of it all. As Robert started explaining she struggled to focus. Her mind seemed adrift. *It's a man's world,* she kept thinking, *and no matter how good I am at my job, the main reason I've gotten this far is my looks. And what happens when I'm no longer pretty?*

"Sing, Sing.... please listen."

"Yes, fine, I--I'll do it," Sing said automatically.

"Do what? I haven't asked you to do anything."

"Well, whatever it is will be fine," she said.

"Do you know what I was talking about?"

"Um, no..."

"Ok, Sing." Robert's voice fell. He got up and began pacing the room. "We are reactivating Blue Star, the Nuclear Rocket program."

"Nuclear!" Sing said. Suddenly her voice sounded worried. "I am not a big fan of nuclear, Robert. Remember where I come from. I've seen what it can do to people. What do you want me to say? Maybe, 'Sounds great, sign me up'? No thanks." Disgust laced her voice.

"I know how you feel." Robert stared at the floor. "Frankly I don't want to do it either, but that photo tells us what needs to happen." He paused. "I lost friends and colleagues to the Blue Star project, so I know the danger. But this time I have the freedom to do it right without anyone second-guessing. Like you, I've learned the dangers of nuclear energy."

Sing didn't say anything for a while. Finally she looked up at him. "Let me tell you my story. As you can imagine, growing up in Japan was tough. Women aren't at all equal there. In some ways the American influence changed that. But now I see that in many ways it didn't. When I first got back there, and stepped off the airplane, I was hoping to see even bigger changes. They'd told me they were going to honor me as one of Japan's greatest female scientists. But as soon as I met the ambassador, it was like we were at an amusement park and I was one of the rides. He was completely straightforward about his intentions. He wanted every thrill he could get out of me."

"Oh, my gosh, Sing, I had no idea. I would have done something had I known. Is that what happened, did you..."

"Did I what?"

"You know, did you... did he make you... I mean, what happened then?"

She looked out the window. "It's not polite for a girl to tell."

Robert got a hold of his emotions, and looked down at a slip of paper on his desk. "Sing, have you ever considered the impact of what we are trying to do here?"

"Is that a trick question?" she demanded. "What are you after?"

In Robert's fingers the slip of paper started feeling like a hot ember. It was they key to the universal mystery: *Are we alone?* He could stand it no longer. "Here, Sing," he said, offering her the paper. "Just take a look."

Sing snatched it from him. As she examined it beads of sweat formed on her brow. She paled, and started to sway. Robert caught her. As Sing steadied herself, she stepped away from him. "Good try, Robert. You'll need more than this to knock me off my feet."

"What do you mean?"

"You know what I mean. You're just using this to make up for abandoning me. How did you get it anyway?"

"Explain your interpretation of it, and then I'll tell you where I got it," Robert said.

She looked him in the eye. She'd recognized the ramifications of what was on the paper almost instantly, but having survived Operation Pin Cushion intact, she wasn't about to let any man dictate her success. "Come on, Robert. I don't have time to play cat and mouse." Suddenly she jumped up from her seat, and darted out of his office. "Robert," she called back to him as she marched down the corridor, "if this is what you say it is, you owe me,"

Robert went to the door and watched Sing's hips swaying gracefully under her lab coat as she walked away from him. He followed. As she headed for the computer lab, he couldn't shake the feeling that she was happy about something. He felt as if he'd passed some sort of test, but he had no idea why.

Sing stopped at her desk, and swept piles of papers and manuals onto the floor, sending a couple sailing back over Robert's head. Stepping into the computer lab, she barked: "Load data reels one-through-fifteen, and direct them through the central computing terminal." When she looked up Robert was standing in front of her. She tapped his chest with her index finger. "If this works, you have a lot of explaining to do."

"Ready, Doctor," came the reply over the speaker.

Sing turned to her desk, keyed in the code and studied her oscilloscope. After a few seconds the wave formation started changing. "Look, look!" she cried, pointing. "That's a vocal track in the signal!" She flipped several switches. "Robert, you see this? A visual track--multiple signal patterns... they might be anything. Even with this code it's going to take months process all the data reels we used just recording that blasted signal. I'm afraid we're going to have to spend a lot more time together. The work demands it."

"Sshhh!" Robert hissed, trying to push her into her seat.

She stood fast. "No. Take me to your house and give me a drink, darling. We need to talk." She walked away.

"Um…hey, wait up," Robert called after her. He trotted to catch up. "You know, it's still morning, right? Only ten-thirty."

"I don't care. I've been working 16-hour days. After I refused to sleep with those men, I thought I was going to be fired. There I am, worried over whether I'm going to be fired, and you hand me this little piece of paper that explains just about everything. I don't even know what day it is."

"Sing, I'm sorry. I had no idea--I wanted so badly to enjoy Washington with you, but they took me other places first." He followed her up and out of the silo. She accelerated.

"Sing, wait!" Robert called, out of breath.

Sing stopped at the top of a flight of stairs. She turned, looked down at him, and said nothing.

Robert halted below her, halfway up. "Sing, there is a lot about you I don't understand. The things you do, things you say… even now I can't figure it out. What's going on in that bright mind of yours? I wish I knew. But I want you to understand something: I will never take anything from you that you've earned. Right now you have my trust and respect."

"But I'm missing something," she said.

Robert looked at her. "What?"

Sing rolled her eyes. "Do I need to give you my 'Doctor Sum' speech?"

"Doctor who? Sum? The one who works in the Math department?"

"That's right. He realizes that if I give eggheads like you a 40-page set of instructions, and you follow them faithfully, adventures with earth women will abound." Sing started to giggle at her own joke, then stopped. "Oh no, you know what this means?"

"I have no idea."

"I've contracted the egghead complex," she said, "and there's only one way to cure it."

"I'm afraid to ask. What is it?"

"Well, if you're going to be like that, I'm not telling you," Sing snapped.

"What? Now I'm interested," Robert admitted.

"It's about time! What are you waiting for? Do your duty, man."

Robert's eyes grew large as he comprehended. "Yes," he said, "in just a few seconds. But I need to figure out..." He trailed off.

"You have no idea, do you?" Her tone was almost compassionate, but her mischief still ruled.

"I need a hint," he begged.

"On the plane you said you wanted us to do something."

His eyebrows arched. "Live together?"

Sing smiled, crooked her finger, and signaled her invitation to join her at the top of the stairs. When he got there she put her arms around him. "Do your duty, Robert."

"I can do that," he said as he kissed her.

With that he dove into the most obvious equation in this fluid, dynamic universe.

Sing grabbed Robert's hand, and they hurried through the lobby. As they passed Peggy's desk, Sing winked at her. "Hold our calls," she said. "Robert and I have an important meeting today."

Peggy winked back and mouthed the word, *meow.*

The drive home was quiet. Robert daydreamed of a life with Sing at its center. He knew this meant his entire future would be one of exquisite chaos.

After they'd parked at his house Sing reached the door first. Robert ran up behind her, but she was already pushing the unlocked door open. There in front of her stood a woman.

"Hello, Dr. Sing," said the woman.

Sing stared, and felt her blood starting to boil.

Just then Robert reached her, and gasped: "Uh, Sing meet, Captain Anna Urisa... Captain Urisa meet Doctor Sing Ann Howell."

Sing gave Robert an icy glance. "Full of surprises, aren't we? Here I thought I was being crowned queen of the house... but you already have one."

"Don't worry Doctor Sing," said Anna. "It is I who am looking for a man."

"Oh? And how do you expect me to help you?" Sing asked.

"I need your help, my men didn't find what we needed when they were here before."

"So it was your people turning everything upside down?" Sing asked.

"Please forgive me. Disguising myself behind rags is not my usual behavior," Said Anna. "I'd expected my people to be more discreet. I should have known better."

Robert broke in. "I decrypted most of your message, Captain. There are so many questions I don't know where to begin. What's the Guild? Where did you come from? What's this 'urgency' your message refers to? I need to know."

"You'll know everything in time, but at the moment I desperately need your help saving my people."

Robert fell silent.

Sing spoke in a businesslike manner. "First you must tell me why you're even here."

"That's complicated, we have a Guild code we must follow. I am breaking every rule just talking to you. Even now you are creating opinions that govern future research. Unlocking our message has exposed you to technological advances that you should not be able to acquire for years, perhaps even generations. By sharing our technology and revealing ourselves to you, I have put us all at risk."

"What do you mean, 'at risk'?"

"Though I can't outright give you our technology, I promise, if you help us, you will benefit."

Sing looked at Anna, and understood that they'd been given the code for a reason, but she wasn't about to say it out loud.

"What do you need from us?" Robert asked.

"That's simple," said Anna. "A ride back to the moon."

Robert knew what that meant: Project Blue Star. It would revive all the strongest themes in his life's work, yet the idea of an atomic rocket challenged and even scared him.

Anna spoke quickly: "We must warn the Guild of our findings. Earth may be at risk. If we can't, there is no telling how much time you may have. Something on my ship destroyed our electrical systems and we couldn't stop it. If I couldn't protect my ship, do you really think you can protect Earth?"

Robert thought for a moment. "You said what's on your ship could be a threat to Earth."

"Yes Robert. More then you know."

"Ok, we will get you to the moon, on one condition."

"Name it."

"Help me rebuild my nuclear rocket."

With their basic terms already stated, the three began talking through the details. They realized that there were no simple answers. Threats were everywhere, even in their solutions. Yet two of these people had just fallen in love, giving them the greatest reason in the universe to succeed. That universe, and all it's great mysteries, lay waiting...

www.ingramcontent.com/pod-product-compliance
Lightning Source LLC
Chambersburg PA
CBHW070757120626
46557CB00002B/639